BY JOHN P. MARQUAND

The Moto Series

YOUR TURN, MR. MOTO
THANK YOU, MR. MOTO
THINK FAST, MR. MOTO
MR. MOTO IS SO SORRY
LAST LAUGH, MR. MOTO
RIGHT YOU ARE, MR. MOTO

Selected Novels

THE LATE GEORGE APLEY
SINCERELY, WILLIS WAYDE

Think Fast, Mr. Moto

Think Fast, Mr. Moto

JOHN P. MARQUAND

LITTLE, BROWN AND COMPANY

BOSTON   TORONTO

REPUBLISHED JULY 1985

Library of Congress Cataloging in Publication Data

Marquand, John P. (John Phillips), 1893–1960.
  Think fast, Mr. Moto.

  I. Title.
PS3525.A6695T39 1985   813'.52   85-7044
ISBN 0-316-54703-4 (pbk.)

BP

Published simultaneously in Canada
by Little, Brown & Company (Canada) Limited

PRINTED IN THE UNITED STATES OF AMERICA

Think Fast,
Mr. Moto

CHAPTER I

IT HAD not taken Wilson Hitchings long to realize that the firm of Hitchings Brothers had its
definite place in the commercial aristocracy of the
East, and that China had retained a respect for mercantile tradition which had disappeared from the
Occidental world. There were still traditions of sailing days and of the pre-treaty days in the transac-
tions of the Shanghai branch of Hitchings Brothers.
The position of its office upon the Bund was enough
to show it. The brass plate of HITCHINGS BROTHERS
was polished each morning by the office coolies so
that it glittered golden against the gray stone façade.
Near by were the venerable plates of JARDINE MATH-
ESON and of the HONG KONG AND SHANGHAI BANK.
The plate of HITCHINGS BROTHERS had the same re-
mote dignity, the same integrity, the same impervi-
ousness to time — which was not unnatural. That
plate had been made when a branch of Hitchings
Brothers, under the control of Wilson's great-grandfather from Salem, had moved up to Shanghai from

3

the factories of Canton during the epoch when the place was little more than a swampy China-coast fishing town.

Reluctantly, but accurately, Wilson Hitchings could feel the venerable weight of that tradition. The involuntary respect which the tradition had engendered in the narrow European world that maintained its precarious foothold in the Orient was accorded to Wilson Hitchings himself, in spite of youth and inexperience, simply because he bore the name. Old white-suited gentlemen whom he never recalled meeting previously would suddenly slap him on the back as though he were an Old China Hand. Leather-faced matrons from British compounds would smile at him archly. Sometimes even an unknown, fat Chinese gentleman calling in the outer office would look at him and smile.

"Mr. Hitchings," the old gentleman would say, "so nice you have come here."

"Gentlemen," someone would say, toward evening at the bar, "this is young Hitchings, just out from America. He doesn't know me but I know him. He looks the way old Will did when he came out. . . . Boy, give Mr. Hitchings a drink. . . . We have to stick together these days. Anything I can tell you, Mr. Hitchings, simply let me know."

It had not taken Wilson Hitchings long to realize that he was a public character by right of birth. He grew to understand that the small shopkeeper and the lowest inhabitants of the International Settlement all knew him and that there is no such thing as privacy in the East. Sometimes late at night strange, ragged rickshaw boys would speak to him, in the limpid pidgin English of the place.

"Marster Hitchings," a strange boy would shout. "Please, I take you home. I know where Marster Hitchings lives."

And sometimes at the street intersections where the pedestrians and the carts and the motors went by in an unending ribbon, the bearded Sikh policeman would bare his white teeth in an unexpected smile.

"All right," the man would say. "All right now, Hitchings Sahib."

He had begun to realize that a part of Shanghai belonged to him, a part of that rich, monstrous, restive, sinful city where so many races dwelt noisily. It belonged to him because a Hitchings had been there ever since foreigners had come. A Hitchings had seen the city grow out of the East, where China, with that adaptability peculiar alone to itself, had absorbed the conveniences of the West and had made them into something genial and mystic and peculiar. The firm of Hitchings Brothers, on the spot it occupied along the Bund, had become a part of the life. The windows of the firm, never entirely clean in spite of diligent washing, looked out like the eyes of cynical old men upon one of the strangest sights in the world. Beside the Bund flowed the yellow treacherous currents of the Whangpoo River; warships and huge liners were moored in the river, the last word of Occidental ingenuity, and past them always drifted brown-sailed junks, almost unchanged since the oldest Chinese paintings. Sampans, propelled by a single sculling oar, plied their ways across the river. Scavengers, in the sampans, fought raucously over ships' garbage; and down on the street beneath, men stripped to the waist struggled like beasts, pulling burdens while limousines passed by. Out of the firm windows one could see all the comedy and tragedy of China struggling in a world of change, all the unbelievable inequality of wealth, ranging from the affluence of fortunate war-lords to a poverty reduced to a limit of existence which no stranger could envisage. It was all beneath the windows, restive and fascinating, something much better accepted than studied.

Wilson Hitchings reluctantly admired his uncle for his cold acceptance of the enigmas which moved about them. Uncle Will Hitchings had grown to accept street riots and homicide as easily as he accepted his whisky-and-soda at the Club, provided dinner was properly and efficiently served as soon as he shouted "Boy!"

"My boy," Uncle Will used to say, "there's one

thing for you to get in your mind — the firm of Hitchings Brothers is an honest firm. It has an excellent reputation upriver. Every Chinese merchant knows us. We seldom lose our customers; you must learn who these customers are; but don't worry much about the rest. Treat our customers politely, but don't mix with the natives. It's confusing to you now. It used to be confusing to me at first, but you'll get used to it. Don't try to speak their language. You can't learn it and it will only make you queer to try. I've seen a lot of nice young fellows who have got queer trying to learn Chinese. Just remember our family has got along on pidgin English. The main thing is to be seen with the right people. I don't care how much you drink if you do it with the right people and in the right place; and don't worry too much about wars and revolutions. Everything is always upset here. All we need is to be sure we get our money, and there's just one thing more — about women. Be sure you don't marry a Russian girl. And get as much exercise as you can, and remember I am broad-minded. Come to me when you're in trouble, remember that nothing will shock me — nothing; and don't forget you have the firm name. I'll see you before dinner at the Club."

It was a strange life, an easy life, and altogether pleasant. In spite of the size of the city, the city was like a country club where everyone of the right sort knew everyone else, where everyone moved in a small busy orbit, surrounded by the unknown, and where everyone was friendly. It did not take him long to realize that it was a responsibility to bear the family name.

"You see," his uncle told him, "we are one of the oldest firms in China and age and name mean a great deal here. I want you to come to dinner to-night. My new cook is very good. I want you to change your cook, he is squeezing you too much. I want you to be sure to be at the Club every afternoon, and I want you to use my tailor. His father and his grandfather have always dressed the Hitchingses."

"Do you think there is going to be trouble up North, sir?" Wilson Hitchings asked.

His Uncle Will looked at him urbanely. His broad, red face reminded Wilson of the setting sun.

"There is always trouble up North," Uncle William said. "I want you to get yourself a new mess-jacket. The one you wore last night didn't fit, and that's more important than political speculation. You had better go to your desk now. I shall have to read the mail. Well, what is it?"

The man who sat in front of the door of William Hitchings' private office — a gray-haired Chinese in a gray cotton gown — entered.

"Please, sir," he said, "a Japanese gentleman to see

8

you — the one who came yesterday." Uncle William's face grew redder.

"My boy," he said to Wilson, "these Japanese are always making trouble lately. They're underselling us all along the line. You may as well sit and listen. How long have you been here now?"

"Six months, sir," Wilson Hitchings said.

"Well," his uncle said, "we have important interests in Japan. You had better begin to get used to the Japanese. Yes, sit here and listen." He waved a heavy hand to the office attendant.

"Show the man in," he said.

Red-faced, white-haired, and growing heavy, William Hitchings sat behind his mahogany table with the propeller-like blades of the electric fan on the ceiling turning lazily above his head. Short as the time had been since he had been sent to China, Wilson could understand that much of his uncle's attitude was a façade behind which he concealed a shrewd and accurate knowledge. He sat there looking about his room with a heavy placid stupidity which Wilson could suspect was part of his uncle's stock in trade. Even his bland assumption of ignorance of Chinese was valuable. His uncle had once admitted, perhaps rightly, that it all gave a sense of confidence, a sense of old-fashioned stability.

It had been a long while since the firm had started

dealing in cargoes of assorted merchandise; and now its business, largely banking, was varied and extensive. The firm was prepared to sell anything up-country through native merchants who had been connected with it for generations, and the firm was the private banker for many important individuals. Wilson could guess that his uncle knew a great deal about the finances and the intrigues of the Nanking Government, although his conversation was mostly of bridge and dinner.

While they waited Uncle William began opening the pile of letters before him with a green jade paper-cutter. Once he glanced at the clock then at the door and then at his nephew. It was three in the afternoon.

"My boy," said Uncle William, "I want you to listen to this conversation carefully and I want you to tell me what you think of it afterwards. I want you to consider one thing which is very important. You must learn to cultivate a cheerful poker face. That is what you are here for, and it will take you years before you can do it."

"You have one, sir," said Wilson.

"Yes, my boy," said Uncle William, "I rather think I have." He laid down his paper-cutter and raised his voice a trifle.

There were footsteps outside the office door. Uncle William looked at the wall opposite him, which was adorned with an oil painting of the first Hitchings factory at Canton, beside which was a Chinese portrait of a stout gentleman in a purple robe seated with a thin hand resting on either knee. It was the portrait of old Wei Qua, the first hong merchant with whom the Hitchingses had dealt. Wei Qua's face was enigmatic, untroubled and serene.

"Now in the races to-morrow," Uncle William said distinctly, "I like Resolution in the third. There are going to be long odds on him to-morrow and he is always good in mud. Yes, I think I shall play Resolution."

The office door was opening and Uncle William pushed back his chair. A Japanese was entering, walking across the room in front of the corpulent Chinese clerk with swift birdlike steps.

"Mr. Moto, if you please," the Chinese clerk was saying.

Mr. Moto was a small man, delicate, almost fragile. His patent leather shoes squeaked slightly as he walked. He was dressed formally in a morning coat and striped trousers. His black hair was carefully brushed in the Prussian style. He was smiling, showing a row of shiny gold-filled teeth, and as he smiled he drew in his breath with a polite, soft sibilant sound.

"It is so kind of you to receive me," he said. "So very, very kind, since I sent my letter such a short time ago. Thank you very, very much."

"The pleasure is all mine," Uncle William said. "Thank you, Mr. Moto." ·

Mr. Moto had handed him a card which William Hitchings took carefully, almost gingerly.

Wilson had already grown to understand that manners in the Orient demanded that a visiting card must be treated with studied respect.

"This is my nephew," Uncle William said. "Mr. Wilson Hitchings, Mr. Moto." Mr. Moto turned toward Wilson swiftly; his eyes and his teeth sparkled.

"Oh," said Mr. Moto — "Oh, your nephew? I am so pleased to meet you, sir, very, very pleased." His English was perfect, his voice was soft and modulated with little of the monotonous, singsong articulation of so many of his race. Mr. Moto's eyes met Wilson's studiedly.

"You have not been here long, I think, sir," he said. "I hope you like it very much. It is so nice to see you. I hope you like Shanghai. It is such a very nice city, is it not?"

"Yes," said Wilson. "I like it very much."

"I am so glad," said Mr. Moto, "so very, very glad."

"Please," said Uncle William. "Won't you sit down, Mr. Moto?"

"Thank you," said Mr. Moto. "Thank you, so very much."

"Wilson," said Uncle William, "pass Mr. Moto the

cigarettes. Will you have tea or whisky, Mr. Moto?"

Mr. Moto laughed genially.

"Ha, ha," said Mr. Moto. "Whisky soda, if you please, because it is an American drink. I have resided in your country. I like it so very, very much."

"Boy!" called Uncle William. "Whisky soda. . . . Here's to you, Mr. Moto." Mr. Moto laughed again.

"Here is looking at you, gentlemen," he said. "That is the American expression, is it not? What beautiful weather we are having!"

"Yes," said Uncle William. "We were speaking about the races. What do you like in the third race, Mr. Moto?"

"What do I like?" inquired Mr. Moto, a shade of bewilderment crossing his face. Then he smiled again. "Excuse," he said. "Now I understand. I do not like any horse in the third race very much." He turned to Wilson still smiling and sipped a little of his whisky. "We are so fond of American sports in Japan," he said. "Ha, ha, we have great sports there. We have tennis and golf and skiing and baseball — such a great deal of baseball. Sports are very, very nice, I like them very, very much. Do you like sports?"

"Yes," said Wilson, "I like them very much."

"I am so glad," said Mr. Moto, "so very, very glad. We shall see you in Japan, I hope."

"Yes," said Uncle William. "I am planning to send

13

him to Tokyo for a while next year. We are breaking him in here now."

"Breaking him in?" said Mr. Moto. "Oh, yes, I understand. That is very nice. You mean he will be a member of the firm — that will be very nice. We admire this firm so very much."

"Thank you, Mr. Moto," Uncle William said. "It is kind of you to say so."

"Thank you," said Mr. Moto, "very, very much." And he took another drink from his glass.

"Wilson," said Uncle William, "give Mr. Moto a light for his cigarette."

And they began to talk again about nothing. The atmosphere was formal, but neither Mr. Moto nor Uncle William seemed to be oppressed by any sense of time. Wilson had been told to listen carefully, but his mind could hit on nothing important. Mr. Moto sat there nervously, politely, chatting about nothing. And then at last he asked a question. He asked it casually, but Wilson could guess what he had come for was to ask that single question.

"I have been looking for a Chinese gentleman," Mr. Moto said. "A gentleman named Chang Lo-Shih, such a very nice gentleman. He is buying some of our bicycles. You remember him, perhaps?"

Uncle William looked at the ceiling.

"Chang Lo-Shih," he said. "No, I am sorry, at the moment I do not remember."

14

"He had business in Manchuria," Mr. Moto said. "At the time of the old Marshal."

"I am sorry," said Uncle William, "I still do not remember. That is getting to be a long while ago. Like so many other American firms, we have closed our offices in Mukden, Mr. Moto. But if you are interested I can look through our files."

"Oh, no," said Mr. Moto. "Please, please no! It is nothing, really nothing."

"Have you been in Manchukuo lately?" Uncle William asked.

"Yes," said Mr. Moto. "It is very, very nice."

"Yes," said Uncle William. "It is a beautiful country."

Mr. Moto took another sip of his whisky.

"But the bandits," said Mr. Moto. "They still make trouble. You read of them in the papers, do you not? I myself had trouble with the bandits."

"I hope it was not serious," Uncle William said.

"Oh, no," said Mr. Moto. "It was nothing. Only a very little trouble." Mr. Moto rose. "You have been so very, very kind to receive me," he said. "Thank you so very, very much."

"It has been thoughtful of you to call," said Uncle William. "Give my regards to the head of your firm when you get home and please come in again, any time at all. It has been a great pleasure to see you, Mr. Moto."

"Thank you," said Mr. Moto, "very, very much." He set down his whisky glass carefully. It was still three quarters full. He bowed and smiled and shook hands.

"Wilson," said Uncle William, "see Mr. Moto to the door."

"Shanghai is a beautiful city," Mr. Moto said. "So very, very many different people."

"They call it the Paris of the East, don't they?" Wilson asked.

"Ha, ha," said Mr. Moto. "That is very good — the Paris of the East! I am so very glad to have met you, Mr. Hitchings. I hope so very much that we may meet again."

Back in his private room, Uncle William was busy opening his letters.

"Well," he asked, "what did you think of Mr. Moto?"

Wilson smiled.

"I thought he was very, very nice," he said.

Uncle William looked at the portrait of Wei Qua. The fan above his head moved its mahogany wings slowly, noiselessly.

"What did you think of the talk?" he asked.

"Nobody said anything," Wilson said.

Uncle William slit another envelope with his green jade cutter, pulled the letter out and unfolded it.

"That's exactly why I wanted you to listen," he

16

said. "You may not know it, but that was a highly important call. Mr. Moto and I knew it. And now I'll tell what I think. You heard him mention Chang Lo-Shih? Let me tell you something — that means that old Chang is meddling in Manchukuo. I said I didn't know him, but I do. It's as good as a warning not to do business with Chang, and I'll tell you something else — Mr. Moto isn't a businessman. Can you guess what he is?"

"No, sir," Wilson said.

"Well, I'll tell you what I guess I think he is," Uncle William said, "and I'll know to-morrow if I'm right. Mr. Moto is a Government agent, and he's after my old acquaintance Chang Lo-Shih; and just you remember this, Wilson: Be careful of Mr. Moto. I'll bet you run into him again and when you do, don't tell him any of the firm's secrets — not that you know any — and don't drink any more whisky than he does, Wilson. Now if you'll wait for five minutes we'll go over to the Club."

"Yes, sir," said Wilson. He sat quietly watching his uncle, aware of his own complete uselessness to cope with such situations. He sat there wondering, not for the first time, whether he would ever understand the complications of the new life he had started. He even wished vaguely that he was back at home and he felt a growing respect for the abilities of his family. The Hitchingses had coped with

China for a hundred years and they could still cope with China. Then a sound from his uncle startled him.

His Uncle William had slammed a paper on the desk.

"By God!" said Uncle William, "that woman still has our name on that gambling house in Honolulu!"

"What woman?" asked Wilson.

"Cancel any engagement you may have," said Uncle William. "You are to dine with me alone tonight." Uncle William mopped his forehead. It occurred to his nephew that he had never seen his uncle look so disturbed, and he knew why — the name of Hitchings was something to be taken very seriously out there in the East.

"Read that letter," said Uncle William, "and then put it in your pocket. I want you to think about it. I'll talk to you about it seriously after dinner."

Wilson examined the letter carefully, because he had learned that the external appearances of a letter often told more about the writer than the contents. It was written on several large sheets of paper, of a good quality, evidently intended for a typewriter, although his uncle's correspondent had written it by hand with a stub pen and blue-black ink. The writing at first glance seemed scrawling and careless but the whole was perfectly legible and each letter was incisive and distinct. He would have known it was a woman's writing even if his uncle had not indicated it. Then it had the lack of discipline of penmanship peculiar to his own generation. The sender's address was embossed on the top of each page by a well-cut die.

"HITCHINGS PLANTATION," the letterhead read, "HONOLULU, T.H."

He remembered afterwards that the letterhead surprised him, since he had never heard there was a plantation anywhere in the world bearing the family name. He mentally contrasted it with the heavily engraved letterhead of the Hitchings firm: "HITCHINGS BROTHERS, BANKERS AND COMMISSION MERCHANTS, HONOLULU, SHANGHAI, CANTON." To anyone familiar with the American vicissitudes of mercantile ventures, during the past century, those words were illuminating enough. They indicated that the Hitchings family had built up and maintained a commercial position which was still strong after nearly all the houses that had started with them had disappeared. The firm letterhead told of the northwest trade and the China trade. It indicated more than clever management. It indicated complete mercantile and banking integrity. Even then Wilson had an intuition that the letter headed "Hitchings Plantation," which he was holding, indicated something entirely different. He felt an instinctive cautious resentment that the family name should be embossed upon it — a resentment which extended to the writer. The letter read: —

Dear Mr. Hitchings, —

I suppose you are a distant relative of mine, since my father sometimes spoke of you when he was alive, but I don't know how we are related. Frankly, I don't much care. Mr. Wilkie, your Branch Manager in Honolulu, advised me to write you personally. That is my only reason for doing it.

Mr. Wilkie has forwarded me several times your offers to buy the house which my father left me and which has always been called "Hitchings Plantation," with exactly as much right as you call your own firm "Hitchings Brothers." He has explained your anxiety to purchase the property from me on the grounds that it is a gambling establishment and that its name is hurting the fine old traditions of your own business. From what I know of your business pursuits, I don't believe that a roulette table can hurt them very much. You have been so anxious to buy me out that I wonder if you have not some other reason. Bankers so seldom tell the real truth.

At any rate, whatever your reason is, this letter is to tell you that you are wasting your time in making me offers. "Hitchings Plantation" is going to remain open as long as I have anything to do with it. There is no reason why I should have any sympathy for your delicacy about the family name. As a matter of fact, I feel that my particular way of earning my living is about as honorable as yours, even if it doesn't pay so well.

I wonder if you remember what happened when my father had financial reverses a few years ago. When he went to his rich relatives and asked for help, he did not even get sympathy. That is why we began having card tables in the house: because we had to do something to get along. People like to come out to the Plantation. There has never been enough disturbance to make the authorities object. When my father died, I put in a roulette table and frankly made it a gambling casino because I had to earn my living. A good many people here sympathize with me, which perhaps you know. You could have helped us once and you didn't. There is no reason why I should help you now — and I won't. I haven't any more use for you than you have for me. You can try to bring legal pressure to bear, if you want to, but I don't think you will. You don't want publicity any more than I do, so I should let the matter drop and let the black sheep of the family alone.

Very truly yours, —

EVA HITCHINGS.

Wilson laid the letter back on his uncle's desk and his uncle did not speak. There was a quality in his silence which told Wilson that it would be just as well not to appear amused, although the letter did amuse him. It referred to circumstances of which he had known absolutely nothing, so that he could think quite freely of the person who wrote it. Evidently, a girl who was angry — yet the anger seemed to him harmless. A gambling house bearing the family name was a circumstance which the older generation might consider more important than did his own. He could even wonder what the place was like and what the girl was like who ran it. He had never realized that there was any branch of the Hitchings family on an island in the middle of the Pacific, and the idea interested him.

His uncle looked at him over the papers on his desk.

"Well, what do you think of it?" his uncle asked.

"I wonder what we did to her father?" Wilson answered. "Who is she? I don't see that it is very important."

His uncle placed the point of his paper knife on the palm of his heavy hand. His face seemed more vacant than usual.

"You must learn not to make snap judgments," his uncle said. "Out here nothing that is important ever seems important, Wilson. I don't like that letter and I don't know exactly why. There has been too much talk about that gambling house. It's getting too well known. People are beginning to associate it with the Bank, but that isn't why I don't like the letter. There is some sort of situation behind it. . . . There is something wrong in Honolulu. . . . You asked me who the girl is. Well, you are having dinner with me. We'll talk about that to-night."

His uncle moved his hands through his letters,

quickly, almost carelessly, and his momentary annoyance was gone; but Wilson knew that something was disturbing him — some unexplained suspicion was disturbing his uncle. The Hitchingses were always a cautious and suspicious family.

CHAPTER II

Iт HAD been his uncle's habit to dine with him quietly, at least three evenings a week, and to talk after dinner of certain aspects of the business. Wilson would sit at such times and listen, fascinated, wondering if he would ever learn it all. Uncle William lived in the family house that had been built in the seventies in a garden behind high compound walls. The house, entirely European, always reminded him of a Chinese copy of a European picture, for in some way China had crept into the architectural plan. Yet there was nothing definite about the house which indicated it. It may have been only the sights and sounds around it. The house was of gray stone, with a gray mansard roof. Inside the furniture was mid-Victorian, and except for the servants there was nothing Oriental in the house.

First there was whisky-and-soda on the back porch overlooking the garden; then, after dinner, they sat on the back porch again, smoking cigars.

"Wilson," Uncle William said, "I think I ought to tell you something."

"What is it, sir?" asked Wilson.

"Frankly," said Uncle William, "when you first came out here I was disappointed in you. You seemed to me shy. You did not seem to be able to mix or to have the human touch; but you're improving, Wilson."

"Thank you, sir," said Wilson. And then he added something which had been on his mind for some time. "It's not easy to be natural when you are a part of an institution."

"No," said Uncle William, "but you are doing better, Wilson. A number of the women at the Country Club have spoken of you in very high terms. There is something about you that women like. I am very glad of that. Do you think you are going to like it here?"

"Yes, sir," said Wilson. "I think I will, when I understand it."

"Boy!" called Uncle William. "Whisky soda." He flicked the ash from his cigar and looked across the garden. It was almost dark by then and the noise from the city all around them was mysterious in the dark.

"I am glad to hear that you are going to like it," Uncle William said, "and I am particularly glad that you have reached no conclusions yet. When you stay out here as long as I have, you will find that it is better to make up your mind about only a very few things. You drink very well, Wilson, and you do not talk too much. I believe that you have got brains. I believe eventually that you can take control of this Branch of Hitchings Brothers."

"Thank you, sir," said Wilson. He knew that it was a great deal for his uncle to say.

"Of course," said his Uncle William, "you have done nothing as yet. You have simply met a few people. I have not bothered you with office routine. I have only tried to help you a little with social values and position. Now I am going to give you something to do. It will be your first job, Wilson. Did you read that letter?"

"Yes, sir," Wilson said.

"Well," said Uncle William, "you are going to call on that cousin of ours in Honolulu. I want you to close that matter up. I haven't time to do it." He looked through the door leading to the main part of the house as though something troubled him. "Boy," he said, "bring me a cigar."

Wilson Hitchings sat up straight. It was not the first time that his uncle had startled him.

"But how do you want me to settle it?" he asked.

Uncle William's voice was bland.

"By using your own judgment," he said. "It's time you had a chance to use it. You can draw on the firm for any amount. I'll leave that up to you."

"But I don't know anything about this," Wilson said.

His uncle flicked the ash from his cigar and stared thoughtfully at the evenly glowing end. "Your remark reminds me that I know very little myself," he answered. "When you have been out here as long as I have, you will find that intuition counts as much as knowledge. The family has always had intuition. Frankly, it's a rather difficult gift to define. I think perhaps you have that gift. A connoisseur can look at a picture which seems correct to a layman, but a connoisseur may have an indefinable sense that something is wrong with its values. Without really knowing anything, it has been dawning on me for the last short while that something is wrong with the values of our Honolulu Branch, although I can give no explicit reason. Business is quiet enough there. The Branch is more of an ornament inherited from the past than a paying proposition. Now, if you will listen to me carefully, I will try to give you a few details. They may explain my unrest when you put them together. Have you ever been to Honolulu, Wilson?"

"No, sir," Wilson said. "I came out here by way of Europe, you remember."

"Of course," said his uncle. "Then you have never seen the Islands. Well, you have something still to

27

see. They are rather close to being South Sea Islands, and for once the travel circulars are right. It is hard to exaggerate their beauty and their climate. The only trouble is that the externals of life are too easy. Men are apt to grow a little soft when life is too easy. I sometimes think that is what is happening to Wilkie."

"You mean our Branch Manager out there?" Wilson asked.

His uncle's talk seemed discursive, almost rambling, but he knew it would pay to listen carefully.

"Yes," his uncle said. "Joe Wilkie. He's been the Branch Manager out there for thirty years now. . . . He's had an easy life; the last time I was there, he had enough leisure for yachting. He has bought one of those Japanese power boats that are used for fishing and has had her made all over as a cruiser. That sort of thing is all right within limits, but outside activities seem to have taken his mind off work. He has been careless in this business about Ned Hitchings' daughter. I wonder; I sometimes think he may have been deliberately careless — not that I have ever seen the girl, and I hadn't seen Ned Hitchings for years before he died. I should like you to watch Wilkie, Wilson. I don't think he has the capacity to be actively dishonest; but watch him, please."

Wilson nodded in obedient agreement.

"I always try to watch," he said. "Who was Ned Hitchings?"

At first Wilson thought his uncle had not heard his question. His uncle was watching him obtusely and carelessly.

"I have seen you watching people," Uncle William said. "It is a habit you mustn't lose, and I hear you can move quickly when it is necessary. They told me there was a fight at Joe's Place last night. A drunken sailor bumped into you."

Wilson could not guess how his uncle had ever heard except that any event, however small, seemed to be public in Shanghai.

"It wasn't anything—" he said. "I suppose I look quieter to people than I really am. There wasn't really much trouble. I rather like Joe's Place."

His uncle appeared to have forgotten the subject at hand but Wilson knew that it was a habit. He knew that his relative was worried.

"Have you ever tried the wheel upstairs?" Uncle William asked. "Joe knows all the gambling tricks from Monte Carlo to Canton. Well—you were asking me about Ned Hitchings. I guess he knew them, too. Ned was a wild boy back at home."

"I never heard of him, sir," Wilson Hitchings said.

His uncle pursed his lips.

"When the Hitchings family drums anyone out

of camp," Uncle William answered, "they don't speak of them to the rising generation. Ned Hitchings is your father's and my third cousin. He had a share in your great-grandfather's trust estate. Your grandfather was executor. When the estate was settled, your grandfather took him into the New York office. Ned and your father and I were younger then. That was before I came out here. Ned used to shock me then. He wouldn't shock me now."

"No," said Wilson. "I don't suppose he would."

"You see," Uncle William explained, "one grows tolerant as one grows older. Even in the Hitchings family. Yes, Ned was quite a boy. He didn't fit well in the office. That money he inherited didn't fit well with him. He married a dancing girl out of one of those Broadway extravaganzas. It rather shocked me then. It wouldn't shock me now. Come to think of it, she was a rather pleasant girl, but it finished Ned. You couldn't have a man like that active in the business. Be careful whom you marry, Wilson, please. Be careful."

"Yes, I will," Wilson answered.

His uncle flicked the ash from his cigar.

"Well," he said. "Ned drifted out to Honolulu and put all his money into a house that he called 'Hitchings Plantation.' Ned always spent his money freely. They had a daughter; then his wife died; then he lost the money. He mortgaged his place. He wrote to your father and me asking us to help him out. We didn't. Maybe we were wrong. . . . That's all. I never thought about the girl until she turned the place into a gambling establishment. Have you never heard of it?"

"No, sir," Wilson said.

"Then I would find out about it, if I were you," said Uncle William. "It seems they want to keep the tourists entertained in Honolulu. The place is called 'Hitchings Plantation' and the authorities are rather partial toward it. Every tourist with sporting proclivities goes straight there from the boat. It's the talk of the world cruises. They are joking about it out here now. They are saying it is part of Hitchings Brothers. It isn't good for business, Wilson. We have been trying for the last six months to buy Ned's daughter out and close the place."

"And she won't sell," said Wilson.

Uncle William shrugged his shoulders.

"You saw the letter," he answered. He glanced over his shoulder toward the open door behind him as though he were listening for some sound.

"Are you expecting a caller, sir?" Wilson asked.

"You are rather quick, aren't you?" his uncle answered. "As a matter of fact, I am; a rather secret caller, and I am not going to do business with him either. . . . Well, you know as much as I do about Hitchings Plantation. I want you to see what is the matter, Wilson. I want you to buy it and get it closed, and you had better rely on intuition. The only thing that has kept our heads above water here is intuition. Don't ask me any more. I have got other things on my mind to-night."

The door behind them creaked. There was a soft pad of slippers on the veranda and William Hitchings' servant, a white-robed figure in the dark, was whispering something softly.

"He is waiting now?" asked Uncle William.

"Yes, marster," the servant said.

Uncle William rose and lighted a fresh cigar.

"Anything else you want to know?" he asked.

"No, sir," Wilson said. "Perhaps I had better find out someone who knows about Hitchings Plantation before I go to bed. It is time I began to put things together."

"Yes, it is time," said Uncle William. "I wish I might help you, but there is a gentleman here to see me. I wonder if you could guess who he is."

"How can I guess, sir?" Wilson asked.

"Think," said Uncle William. "Try to think carefully about what happened this afternoon."

"Do you mean that Mr. Moto is calling?" Wilson asked. He could not see his uncle's face, but he guessed that his uncle was smiling.

"No," his uncle said; "not exactly, but Mr. Moto probably has someone waiting in the street outside.

No, Wilson, not Mr. Moto. Mr. Chang is calling — the gentleman who once had business interests in Manchuria. And I can guess what he wants. He wants me to help him with some more business. Well, I won't. There's a point where one must stop. I'll see you in the morning, Wilson."

As Wilson Hitchings walked down the hallway to the front of his uncle's house, he did not realize that his uncle was not behind him until he was close to the front door. Near it on the left, the door to his uncle's study was ajar and only a dim light was burning in the hallway. As Wilson passed the study, the door opened wider and a voice spoke softly.

"Mr. Hitchings." The voice was so quiet and assured that Wilson was neither startled nor surprised.

"Yes?" he said, and turned to the study door, to find he was facing a man whom he had never seen. The man was a broad-shouldered Chinese, past middle age, dressed in gray, European clothes. He had close-cropped iron-gray hair. Wilson had been in the Orient long enough by then to realize that all Chinese did not look alike. He was even able to identify certain types. The man, he concluded, because of his delicate, rather nervous features, was from the South rather than from the North of China. His dress and his manner showed that he was a man of ability. Just at that moment, the Chinese gentleman looked very much surprised. He was staring at Wilson, unblinking, almost suspiciously, and he had forgotten to be polite.

"Excuse me," he said. "I thought you were Mr. Hitchings, sir."

Wilson smiled.

"You mistook me for my uncle, sir," he said. "But I am Mr. Hitchings, too." Wilson was astute enough to perceive that the man was very much relieved. He smiled also and held out his hand, a slender, delicate hand.

"I am so glad," he began. "I thought you were a stranger." And then Wilson heard his uncle's heavy step.

"Yes, it's my nephew, Mr. Chang," his uncle was saying, "and you need not worry. My nephew knows how to keep his mouth shut. Our family has always been tight-lipped with customers."

Mr. Chang's smile grew broader, and he bobbed his head in a quick, nervous bow.

"Yes, indeed, I know," he said. "That is why I have come to you to-night, and why I hope so much that I may interest you."

His uncle's car was waiting outside the wall and Wilson Hitchings told the driver to take him home. He sat looking through the window at the city streets which for the most part in that quarter were like the streets of a Continental European city. But there was an intangible addition, something exotic that made him ill at ease. The shops and the faces on the streets were like that day: superficially correct but inwardly bewildering.

"There was something wrong about to-day," Wilson Hitchings said to himself, yet he could not have told exactly what was wrong. It was only the inherited intuitive sense which had kept his family afloat for several generations that told him things were not exactly right. And there had been a curious inflection in his uncle's voice, when he had spoken of Mr. Chang, which had been sharper than amusement. What disturbed Wilson Hitchings most was his utter lack of knowledge and his consequent complete inability to give a reason for his uneasiness. That unrest of his was as enigmatic as the tension which surrounded the city of Shanghai. He had felt that disquiet more than once when he had been by himself doing nothing. In the back of his mind there was always the impression of mysterious things happening inland that came out in garbled accounts in the local press. Shanghai had seemed more than once, as it seemed to him to-night, an impermanent safety square in some enormous game — a city which might disappear overnight. The clubs, the offices, all the people of his race, were only there on sufferance. They were probably doing nothing permanent, but that impermanence made it interesting. His family had ridden successfully on the turbulence of China. He wondered if he could do it. He wondered if his life would be a series of errands such as the one his uncle had assigned to him that night. His uncle had thought nothing of sending him on a six weeks' journey and, curiously, the implications of that journey did not worry him as much as the unknown implications around him. At least there was something definite in what he was going to do.

His rooms had the austere simplicity of his family's house at home. He had not taken many things with him when he had been sent to the East, although he knew that he would be there for a long while, perhaps indefinitely. He had brought perhaps a hundred volumes which now stood on plain white shelves. There was a family Bible and some old books on travel and navigation. There were some pictures on the wall, all of which had to do with the family — one was a faded photograph of the old square Hitchings house in Salem which had been torn down fifty years ago. There were framed photographs of the Hitchings family portraits, whose faces were like reflections of his own face in an oddly distorted mirror. On the whole, they were soothing faces, both intellectual and strong. And he was proud of them; the family had always been proud of its ancestry. He had been used to a simple life at home, and he had not yet overcome a sense of surprise to find his

Chinese servant ready and waiting when he came home at night.

"Zsze," he said to his servant, "you must get your accounts ready. In a few days I am going on a jour ney."

"Yes, marster," the servant said. "Upcountry, marster?"

"No," Wilson told him. "I am going to Honolulu just for a while."

"Oh, yes, marster," the man said; and then he turned to the table and picked up a card. "A gentle-man — he came to call on you this evening."

"What sort of a gentleman?" Wilson asked.

"A Japanese gentleman," the man said. "He was very sorry you were out. He left his card."

Wilson took the card, read it, and placed it in his wallet. It was one of those business cards to which he had already grown accustomed. On one side were characters, on the other was a European name.

"I. A. Mото" the printing read, and beneath was written in pencil: *"So sorry you were out. I hope to see you soon."*

The inscription on the card amused him, but what impressed Wilson most was the accuracy of his Uncle William's prophecy. He recalled that his uncle had said that Mr. Moto would probably try to meet him. Although he had the gift of an orderly mind which could set aside a train of thought and turn readily to another, and though he understood that Mr. Moto was no affair of his, he did not feel like sleep. Intuitively he had the sense that something was happening in Hitchings Brothers. Both Mr. Chang and his uncle had been obviously ill at ease.

When his servant had gone, he picked up a book to read; — a translation by Gilbert Murray of Euripides' "Medea." He began reading the play, purely for conscientious reasons, and because he had brought the volume with him, hoping sometime to read it; but when he reached Medea's first speech to the women of Corinth, the words began to hold him. The bitterness and the anger of that woman, whom he had always considered a pleasant girl in Hawthorne's "Tanglewood Tales," and Euripides' own knowledge of the depth of a woman's mind, filled him with reluctant wonder. There was the conviction of universal tragedy in the bitterness of Medea. Was it possible, he wondered, that all women possessed this latent bitterness? It had certainly not been manifest in his own relations with the girls he had met at home. They had been nice girls, happy girls, and their mothers had been contented and poised. Then, much as he deplored the conduct of Jason, in that it differed rather strongly from his own personal standards, it occurred to him that there was much in Jason which was universal also, and there was too much of Jason's psychology which he could under-

38

stand. The Hitchingses had always been looking for the Golden Fleece. There was something of the spirit of Jason in all the Hitchingses — the same restiveness — the same relentlessness.

Vaguely, and inaccurately, he could identify himself with those pages of Euripides. Somewhere in the night sounds outside his room, the Greek chorus was singing a noiseless, mysterious song that was ringing in the background of his thoughts. He, himself, had been selected to deal with a bitter and a probably unscrupulous woman who was using the family name despitefully, because of resentment. Wilson sighed and turned a page of his book. He was logical enough and frank enough with himself to understand that he was not well equipped to cope with such a problem. He had never been successful with the sort of woman whom he visualized — the adventurous type; and undoubtedly, the proprietress of a gambling house would be exactly that. On the whole, he could not understand why his uncle had said that he was the sort that women liked.

"Unless I am perfectly safe," he said to himself. "That is probably the reason."

The evening was still young and it did no good to read. He could not compose himself for reading because of his own uneasiness. He called for his servant to get him a motor and a driver and walked out into the warm, noisy street.

"Joe's Place," he said to the driver. He wanted to find out more about Hitchings Plantation before he went to sleep and he knew that Joe Stanley was probably the one to tell him. The car moved into the dark city, through streets of twinkling electric signs, more effective than any he had ever seen, perhaps because of the Chinese characters depicted on them in red and green and blue. Joe's Place was in the French concession, on a noisy street, lined with restaurants and cabarets. There was an American bar on the lower floor, with tables and music. There were gambling rooms upstairs. Joe Stanley, himself, was standing near the bar and Wilson wondered, as he often had before, what had brought Joe Stanley to Shanghai to end his days. It was a story which Mr. Stanley never told.

Although he must have been in his middle sixties, he was remarkably well preserved, a soft-spoken courteous American, like a character in a Bret Harte novel. Wilson had seen him more than once, and each time he had learned something new but vague about Mr. Stanley's past.

Mr. Stanley took a cigar from the corner of his mouth and gave Wilson a friendly nod.

"Going upstairs to play?" he asked.

"No, thanks," said Wilson. "Not to-night."

"Well, I'd go upstairs, if I were you," said Mr. Stanley.

40

But Wilson sat down at a small table near the bar.

"I am just going to stay long enough to have a glass of beer," he said. He had to speak loudly to be heard above the noise of drinkers at other tables and of patrons by the bar. "Won't you join me, Mr. Stanley?"

Mr. Stanley sat down next to the table and pulled his yellow vest straight.

"You know I never drink," he said. "I wish you wouldn't sit down here to-night. There's too many rough boys here."

"I won't be here more than a minute," Wilson said. "Have you ever heard of Hitchings Plantation in Honolulu, Mr. Stanley?"

"Yes, son," Mr. Stanley said. "I've heard of it. Why do you ask me?"

"The name," said Wilson. "I was interested. That's all."

"That's funny," Mr. Stanley said. "There was a party in here talking of it, this afternoon. That isn't why you are asking, is it?"

"How do you mean?" Wilson asked him.

"Nothing," said Mr. Stanley. "Nothing. A Russian named Sergi was talking of it this afternoon too. Does that mean anything to you, son? He was in here with a Chinese businessman named Chang Lo-Shih. They tell me they play for high stakes there.

There is a croupier named Pierre — but maybe you know it already, don't you, son?"

Wilson sipped his beer carefully and tried to think, but he could not understand Mr. Stanley's attitude. It presupposed a knowledge which he did not possess. Mr. Stanley's eyes had grown narrow, and he was smiling faintly, mockingly.

"Why do you think I should know?" Wilson asked. "I have never been to Honolulu."

"No?" said Mr. Stanley. "But your name is Hitchings, isn't it? I don't know what you are aiming at, Mr. Hitchings, but you don't get me dragged in. I'm too wise and I'll keep still — so don't you worry. There is Sergi sitting over there." He nodded across the room, and Wilson followed the direction of his glance. A man with a pale, waxen face was sitting alone at the table, staring at an empty glass. A cigarette drooped listlessly from between his lips. "You know Sergi, don't you, Mr. Hitchings?"

"No," said Wilson. "I don't. I came here to ask you a simple question and I don't know what you are driving at."

"No?" said Mr. Stanley. "Listen, son, it's getting late and it's time you was in bed. If you want to know about Hitchings Plantation, ask Mr. Chang, not me. I'm not taking a hand in this. Do you get me, son?"

"No," said Wilson. "I don't."

Mr. Stanley rose.

"It don't matter if you don't," he said. "I know when to keep my mouth shut. No one will get anything out of me. What I know won't hurt a soul. Are you glad of that, son?"

"I still don't know what you mean," Wilson said.

Mr. Stanley held out his hand.

"Put it there, son," Mr. Stanley said. "You haven't been out here long, but if I was running a big enough show, I'd have you in it. You're right to be looking out, but I'm not going to blab what I know to any Japanese. Understand me, son?"

"No," said Wilson patiently; "but I don't suppose you'll explain."

"That's what I'm telling you, son," Mr. Stanley answered. "You can sleep easy and not worry about me. That Jap has been here asking about Hitchings Plantation, not an hour ago."

"What Jap?" asked Wilson.

"You know it already, son," said Mr. Stanley, gently. "A guy named Mr. Moto, and he didn't get a damn word out of me. It's all right, son, go home and go to sleep. I'm not talking, understand? Good night."

"Good night," said Wilson, and he walked out to the street. Mr. Stanley's manner, the whole conversation, puzzled him; but one thing had stopped him asking more. There was only one thing he understood — that Mr. Moto had been very busy, and he could not tell why. He decided to keep the matter to himself until he found out why. He decided not to tell his uncle. He had been told to do the job himself. There was one implication that had been clear enough. For some reason that he did not know as yet, Mr. Stanley had thought he was completely conversant with a situation which he had only heard of that evening. His Uncle William had been right again. There was something wrong with Honolulu. He was sure of it that night. . . .

CHAPTER III

SINCE Wilson Hitchings had been taught to be methodical in dress and in thought and in action, he approached the problem before him methodically. The first thing he did the morning he landed in Honolulu was to call on Mr. Joseph Wilkie, the Manager of the Hitchings Brothers Branch. He walked up a broad street slowly, dressed in tailored white, like a traveler accustomed to the tropics, but he looked around him curiously because it was the first time that he had seen these islands. They had seemed from the ship like a background of a stage. Even when he was safe on land, walking through the warm bright sunlight, the place did not seem any more real than his errand. He still carried in his mind his first view of the city, from the water, with the serrated ridges of volcanic mountains behind it. He could remember the soft fresh springlike tones of green, the blueness of the water, the bronze bodies of boys swimming beside the slowly moving ship, the giant pineapple rising above a canning factory

45

on the waterfront, and the civic tower with the word "Aloha" written on it and the notes of the band playing Hawaiian music. The docking of the ship had been arranged with a theatrical skill which was characteristically American, but there was more than that. There had been something of the old spirit of the islands in that landing. When the first ships had entered that harbor natives must have been swimming beside them, and there must have been music; there must have been flowers. He could never forget that impression of flowers which stout Hawaiian women in gingham dresses were holding out for sale. A trade wind was blowing, moving through coconut palms, and the waterfront was clean and beautiful.

The offices of Hitchings Brothers were in a new yellow stucco building, with palm trees growing in a plot of strange stiff grass beside the door. Inside, the offices were cool and airy and no one seemed in a hurry, not even when Wilson Hitchings handed his card to a man of his own age, also dressed in white.

"Does Mr. Wilkie expect you?" the man asked.

"No," said Wilson. "I don't think he knows I'm coming."

The manager's room was comfortable, like the managers' rooms in all the Hitchings branches. There was a homelike familiarity in the decoration as far as Wilson Hitchings was concerned that made him feel pleasantly sure of himself; but the assurance left him when he examined the man who was waiting for him there. On the trip out, with the meager information at his disposal, Wilson had tried to construct an imaginary Mr. Wilkie — a bad practice, he learned in later times, since imagination hardly ever coincided with fact. His uncle had told him to watch Mr. Wilkie, and he watched; but his first glance showed that Mr. Wilkie was different from anything he anticipated. Wilson could perceive no sinister traits in the man before him — in fact nothing to attract his attention. There was only one thing which particularly impressed him. It had been his uncle's idea that Mr. Wilkie should receive no warning of his visit, and it was clear that Mr. Wilkie was surprised and upset, almost unduly upset for such a circumstance, although his lack of composure seemed due largely to hurt pride.

"Good morning, sir," said Wilson. "My uncle said there was no need to cable."

Mr. Wilkie was standing up in the cool shady room. He was a thin iron-gray-haired man, dressed in tropical white. His face was deeply tanned; his eyes were brown. Something about him indicated an emphasis on dress that came of a preoccupation with personal appearance. There seemed to be a fussiness in his manner, the rather provincial fussiness of a man conscious of his position. There was

47

an effort at façade that went with his clothes and with William Hitchings' account of Mr. Wilkie's cruising boat. It seemed to Wilson that the older man was making a distinct effort to conceal an emotion of annoyance, but annoyance was written in the curve of his close-cut gray mustache. He seemed to be saying silently: "I'm an important man, in an important position. You had no right to come here without telling me. This upsets me very much."

It was largely that annoyance which Wilson noticed, combined with surprise, but there might have been something else.

"It's a great pleasure to see you, of course," Mr. Wilkie said, "the very greatest pleasure. There's nothing like a surprise, is there? A pleasant surprise? How are your uncle and your father? You look like them, Mr. Hitchings. If I had known that you were coming, I should have arranged to have you stay at my house, of course. You'll excuse my not asking you now, won't you? I can't imagine why no one sent me word."

"They thought it wasn't necessary," said Wilson smoothly, and he saw Mr. Wilkie raise his eyebrows. "My uncle asked me to give you this letter. He said it would explain everything."

Mr. Wilkie read the letter attentively, holding it between his carefully tended fingers, while Wilson sat and watched him. As Mr. Wilkie read, his lips tightened, as though repressing an exclamation, and Wilson heard him catch his breath. Then Mr. Wilkie glanced at him curiously and smiled.

"So they're still worried about poor Eva's plantation," he remarked. "I hoped I had made my position clear about it, but I'm afraid I didn't. This has been embarrassing for me, Mr. Hitchings. I can hardly tell you how embarrassing. It hurts to be considered so inefficient in a negotiation that a younger man is sent out; but perhaps it's the best way. I'm very glad to wash my hands of it, Mr. Hitchings, and leave it all to you."

"I'm sure no one meant to offend you," Wilson said. He was thinking even as he spoke that there was something devious in Mr. Wilkie's glance. His intuition was telling him something. It was like his uncle's thought that something was not right. "I didn't ask for this job myself. The whole thing is new to me."

"Yes," said Mr. Wilkie, "I suppose it is. I'll be glad to discuss your plans with you. I'm here to do anything I can to help. I suppose you'll want to see Eva this afternoon."

Wilson sat impassively while Mr. Wilkie spoke. When he answered, he was still trying to read what was in Mr. Wilkie's mind. Although he could put his finger on nothing definite, there was something strange in the air. It occurred to him that no one was natural when Hitchings Plantation was mentioned. Mr. Wilkie was smiling faintly.

"You'll know her better when you're through," he added.

"I'm sure I will," said Wilson slowly.

"Yes," said Mr. Wilkie with the same faint smile, "I'm sure you will."

There was a pause, and then Wilson spoke deliberately.

"It sounds as though you'd like a ringside seat when I see her. Would you, Mr. Wilkie?"

"Yes," said Mr. Wilkie. "You'll excuse me. It's not personal; but, frankly, I should rather enjoy it."

Wilson sat impassively, because he found that impassiveness helped in any interview, and he watched Mr. Wilkie carefully.

"I think I should rather see the Plantation first," he said. "I suppose it will be running to-night? Could you arrange that I get a card? I should rather go there without anyone's knowing who I am."

Mr. Wilkie smiled again, and his smile was polite but not reassuring.

"Nothing is easier than a card, Mr. Wilson," he said, "though I am afraid that Eva will know exactly who you are."

"Why?" asked Wilson. "Unless someone tells her?"

"No one will need to tell her," Mr. Wilkie said. "She will only need to look at you. You are the image of her own father when he first came to the Islands. You have the same narrow face, the same eyes, the same build, the same hands. Anyone would know you for a Hitchings."

"Thanks," said Wilson. He kept his glance concentrated steadily, rather disconcertingly, on Mr. Wilkie's face. "Now you'd better tell me something else."

"Certainly," said Mr. Wilkie, "anything I can."

Wilson leaned forward in his chair. His Uncle William had been a good teacher and he endeavored to imitate his Uncle William's urbanity.

"Mr. Wilkie," he said, "since I have been here you have made me feel conscious of a certain reserve on your part. It surprises me a little. Your manner is not entirely friendly. I think you had better tell me why."

Mr. Wilkie's face grew red; for a moment he looked almost astonished.

"You are speaking rather frankly, aren't you?" he said. "I haven't the slightest intention to offend you."

Wilson paused a moment before he answered, and he had the satisfaction of believing that Mr. Wilkie no longer looked upon him as wholly incompetent.

"I did not say you offended me," he answered. "I said it seemed to me that your manner was unfriendly and then I asked you why. It still seems to me a fair question. We are both employed by Hitchings Brothers, Mr. Wilkie."

Mr. Wilkie's face grew redder.

"You Hitchingses think you own the earth, don't you?" he inquired. The irritability was surprising to Wilson, but it told him what he wished to know — that Mr. Wilkie did not like the family. He felt himself growing cooler in the face of Mr. Wilkie's anger.

"Not the earth, Mr. Wilkie," he said, "but we do control the stock of Hitchings Brothers. That's why you can't blame me for being somewhat surprised."

Mr. Wilkie shrugged his shoulders. Now that he no longer had to conceal his animosity, Mr. Wilkie seemed almost relieved. The lines in his tanned face relaxed as he leaned across the desk.

"You've never been here before, have you?" he asked. "Or you wouldn't be surprised. I've lived here for thirty years, and Ned Hitchings was one of my best friends. I've always known Eva Hitchings, everyone has always known her, and everyone knows what his family did when Ned Hitchings lost his money. He was a fine man — everyone loved Ned; and you can get me fired if you want for saying it."

Wilson Hitchings rose. "If you'd told me that in the first place, I wouldn't have taken so much of your time," he said. "You have a perfect right to your own views, Mr. Wilkie. If you had told my father he would not have held it up against you. But, under the circumstances, I think it would be better if I arranged matters by myself." Mr. Wilkie arose also and his manner had changed.

"That's very fair of you," he said.

"Thank you," said Wilson. "I hope you have always found us fair; at any rate that's all I mean to be here. I mean to be fair to Eva Hitchings, too. You can tell her so if you want to."

Mr. Wilkie cleared his throat.

"There's one thing that you ought to know," he said. "We've a rather small society here, and, being so far away, we are a rather close corporation. Ned Hitchings was very popular. You'll find that everyone takes his side here, and his daughter's side. You will find the Hitchings Plantation is rather universally accepted if only because everyone feels that your family has been unfair."

"I am glad to have you tell me so," said Wilson. "You mean I won't be very welcome?"

"I'm afraid not," said Mr. Wilkie, "and Eva won't close the Plantation because the Hitchingses want her to."

"Well," said Wilson, "don't think of it further, Mr. Wilkie, and I'll say nothing about it."

Mr. Wilkie looked incredulous.

"You won't?" he said.

"No," said Wilson, "why should I? You have a perfect right to your own opinion."

Mr. Wilkie looked at him hard.

"I guess," he said, "they've sent a clever man out."

"Don't say that, Mr. Wilkie," Wilson answered. "I only say what I think, that's all."

"Wait!" said Mr. Wilkie. "Don't go. Won't you stay for lunch at the Club?" Wilson Hitchings shook his head.

"No," he answered, "thank you just as much. I'd better stand by my side of the family. That's all that is worrying us — the family. I'll settle this without troubling you again. Good-by, Mr. Wilkie."

Wilson walked out into the bright street, but the sun no longer seemed warm or pleasant. He was not angry, but he was surprised — surprised because he was used to being treated cordially, yet here in one of the branches of the family's office he had met with a curious reception. He had been told that he would not be liked because his family had been unkind to a girl named Eva Hitchings, and he, as a symbol of the family, was to take the blame for this unkindness. He walked back toward the pier where he had left his bags — solitary, puzzled. The sights on the street registered on his mind half mechanically; the faces he saw bespoke of a mixture of races from all sides of the Pacific Ocean; the flowers in the park by the waterfront, like the people on the streets, had been gathered from the ends of the earth to bask in that springlike air. There was nothing which he saw that was not pleasant. Another time he might have enjoyed it more, but just then there seemed to be something sinister in the brilliance of the flowering trees, in the softness of the wind, in the scent even there in the city, of sea spray and of flowers.

"There is something that isn't right," Wilson was saying to himself. He was not thinking of the city, because the city was beautiful; he was thinking rather of something in his own mind. There was an intuitive uneasiness in his thought, a sense not exactly of danger, but of impending difficulties.

Nevertheless he always remembered a good deal of that day with pleasure, although his thoughts kept obtruding themselves on what he saw. There was an automobile at the pier waiting to be hired, and he selected it because it was an open car. It was driven by a coffee-colored boy in his shirt sleeves, who wore a wreath of flowers around the band of his felt hat.

"I want to hire you for the day," Wilson said. "I shall want to see the Island, but first I'll go to the hotel."

He went to one of the largest hotels on Waikiki Beach, whose name he had often heard travelers mention — a huge building, in a grove of ancient coconut palms, whose leaves rattled hollowly in the trade breeze. The clerk read his name carefully while he registered but he made no comment. It occurred to Wilson that after all the name of Hitchings was not necessarily peculiar.

"If there is anything we can do to help you enjoy yourself, sir," the clerk said, "be sure to let us know, because that's a part of our business. There's the beach, of course, outside, and we can arrange to get you a car from the Golf Club. If there is anything else you want to do be sure to let us know."

Wilson hesitated, looked at the clerk and smiled.

"I've heard there is another club, here," he said, "called 'Hitchings Plantation.' If it isn't asking too much, could you get me a card for that this evening?"

The clerk smiled back at him. "Certainly," he said. "There will be a card waiting for you by dinnertime. Don't mention it, the pleasure is all ours."

Wilson motored through the city that afternoon and out into the hills, as thousands of other tourists have done before him. He was familiar enough with the Hitchings Brothers' history to know something of the history of the city, and he had enough imagination to see the past as it mingled with the present. It amused him as it had in Shanghai to realize that a Hitchings had been there in the beginning even before the wooden mission house had been set up on the spot where it still stood, close to the old coral stone church. That white clapboarded prim New England house had been carried in sections around Cape Horn in the hold of a sailing vessel. It had been, to all intents and purposes, the first house on the Islands, standing among the thatched huts of the natives. The huts were gone, but the mission house still stood and the palace of the Hawaiian kings faced it across the street, and there was the courthouse and the statue of King Kamehameha, with his spear and his feathered cloak, and then the buildings of a modern city with shaded streets of bungalows beyond them. The city was like its history, partly peaceful, partly exotic, partly tolerant, partly strange.

Wilson leaned forward and touched the driver on the shoulder.

"I should like to see Hitchings Plantation," he said. "Will you drive past it, please?" The boy nodded and smiled. He had been talking, describing the sights as they moved by them, and Wilson listened idly to his words.

"King Street. . . . Post Office. . . . Library. . . . Chinese temple. . . . Alexandra Park. . . . Banyan trees. . . . Monkey-pod trees. . . . Shinto Temple. . . . Punch Bowl. . . . High School. . . . King's graveyard. . . . Kukui trees. . . ."

The words moved by dreamily like the sights of the city. The road was leading into the hills and then into a valley bordered by high mountain peaks where rich green vegetation grew on black lava cliffs and ended above them in a mist of low hanging clouds. The valley itself was as rich and green as the Elysian Fields. The driver turned to him and smiled.

"Lovely place," he said.

"Yes," said Wilson, "lovely place."

They were evidently passing through a rich residential section where houses stood on wide lawns behind hibiscus hedges. The car turned to the right down a narrow road and then the sun was gone. There was a light sprinkle of rain.

"Liquid sunshine," the driver said. "We call it liquid sunshine. You see it stops so soon." The car was slowing down. They had reached the end of the branch of the road and he was pointing straight ahead.

"Hitchings Plantation," the driver said.

It was late afternoon by then, an hour which was very close to sunset. The driver was right for the flurry of rain in the valley had been over in a moment leaving the air moist, soft and clean and full of the scent of flowers. Now that the car had slowed down, he was aware of a sense of solitude such as he had not felt all day. They had left the complexities of the city which formed one of the crossroads of the world and were stopping in a cleft between high, dark, green hills whose peaks rose mistily into a sky that was growing reddish with the sunset. Except for the house which was standing where the road ended he could believe that this part of the valley had hardly ever changed. The wildness and isolation of older days hung over it mistily. Wilson Hitchings remembered feeling cold, not entirely because the sun was going down or because of that touch of rain. The Island had changed from a distant, pagan paradise of gods and drums to an outpost of a nation that was half a fortress, half a garden. The missionaries had come to bring the word of God to a childlike trusting people, and the traders had come, and the whaling fleet and the French, and the Russians and the English. The fields had been planted with sugar cane, riches such as no one had ever dreamed of had flowed in. The beaches had become a playground. The city had become a carpet of twinkling lights, but the valley had not changed. It was growing sad and shadowy, a tropical island valley brooding over a simple past. The steep hills seemed to Wilson Hitchings to be waiting, waiting for a time when the vanity of man was gone and when the strong trees and vines would march from down the mountains again into the clearings.

"Hitchings Plantation," the driver said politely, "a lovely place."

"Yes," Wilson said, "a lovely place." He was thinking of the ironies of life. He had reached the spot toward which he had traveled a good many thousand miles and now he gazed at it somberly. The road had ended in a valley stopping at a driveway, flanked by two tall posts that bore the name newly painted, "Hitchings Plantation." The house stood on a lawn that was dotted with fantastic branching trees — a rambling wooden house that had been built in the style of the South at home. He could understand its name as soon as he saw the house — there was a high pillared portico, there were wings and verandas. When he saw it he could understand what Ned Hitchings had done with his money. He had sunk it all prodigally into one estate; it was simple enough to see what had happened afterwards, because the house and the grounds above it gave an impression of desuetude and of disrepair. Ned Hitchings' money had gone into the house and now there was no more money. A building could not last long in that genial climate without upkeep. The grass about it was unkempt, shrubbery was growing wildly against the white wall, the paint was growing dingy, the shutters were sagging.

"They play roulette every night," the driver said. "You want to go inside?"

"No," said Wilson, "not now. I'll go back to the hotel."

He did not say what was in his thoughts, that the loneliness of the hills was in that house and vanished hopes. Something caught at his throat, because it must have been a gallant place once. Then another thought was running through his mind.

"Anything might happen there," Wilson said to himself, "anything might happen."

Then they were going through the outskirts of the city back to the hotel on the beach where music was playing. They were passing along a street which might have been in the Orient. There were open-front Chinese shops where dried fish and parasols and cloth were out for sale. There was a rich smell of cooking and of bean oil — there were rice cakes on the counters, the streets echoed with the notes of Oriental voices, and someone was singing in high falsetto notes. The dark was coming down quickly like a curtain, blotting out the contradictions of that city that was neither East nor West.

"All kinds of people here," the driver said. "Japanese, Chinese, Filipinos, all kinds of people."

"Yes," said Wilson, "all kinds of people." The darkness made the place mysterious and he stood for a while on the hotel lawn beneath the palm trees looking at the sea. It occurred to him that he had never felt so lonely. He was thinking of the valley and of the house.

The clerk gave him his card to the Hitchings Plantation Club and he put it in his pocket and then he went up to his room, a large room overlooking the sea. He unlocked the door and turned on the

61

light and then he noticed a piece of paper lying on the carpet. Wilson picked it up and bent over it frowning.

It was a plain slip of paper with a single line of typewriting upon it. It had evidently been pushed beneath the crack of his bedroom door.

"You look healthy," the paper said; *"if you want to keep healthy, keep away from Hitchings Planta tion."*

He could hear the soft noise of the surf outside and he could smell that strange sweet smell of sea spray and flowers — all these made the note in his hand utterly incongruous. For the first time in a long while he felt his heart beat fast. There was no doubt that the message was intended for him. There was no doubt that the message was a threat. He folded the paper carefully, opened one of his bags, and took out his evening clothes. He moved deliberately and thoughtfully, but his mind was filled with an incredulous sort of wonder. For the first time in his life he was entirely alone at the mercy of his own resources with no one to lean upon for advice or help. For once in his life he was aware that his family name and his connection was something on which he could not lean. He was surrounded by ill-wishers. The note had taught that much, and more than that it had made him understand that this ill will was not entirely passive.

He tried to keep his thoughts calm. The family had always been logical. The significance of the message puzzled him. If it had been intended to frighten him its psychology was very poor, because the note had aroused in him a streak of stubbornness of which he had never dreamed. He was amazed at his own anxiety to get to Hitchings Plantation now that he had received the message. As he stood before the mirror arranging his tie he noticed that his face looked pale and that his eyes were unusually bright. He was wondering where the message had come from. Then he remembered that Honolulu was only a small town as far as his own race was concerned. His name had been on the ship's list and anyone might know him. Mr. Wilkie himself had intimated that anyone might recognize him who was familiar with the Hitchingses — he had the same long nose, the same narrow forehead, the same deep-set eyes, the same large tranquil mouth. Wilson Hitchings stared at himself thoughtfully in the mirror. On the whole the sensation that he was entirely alone was not wholly unpleasant.

"I can probably take care of myself," his mind was saying. "The family always have." The idea of the family was reassuring — it had always reassured him when he thought of his family.

The orchestra in the hotel dining room was playing Hawaiian music, the waiters were Japanese in trim white uniforms. The diners as far as he could gather were all strangers like himself, pleased with the music and with the sea outside. It was like a tranquil June night at home. Against the background of the sea and palms there was a new significance in the music. There was a lingering sadness in it — the echo of old days — the echo of the voices of a dying race. A large man in evening clothes stopped by Wilson's table. Even before he spoke, Wilson guessed who he was.

"Good evening, Mr. Hitchings," the man said. "I am the manager. We are all pleased to have you here. Hitchings is an old name on the Islands."

"And I am new on them," Wilson said. "Won't you sit down for a moment, sir? You have a name for people like me, haven't you — a native name?" The manager seated himself and smiled, the patient smile of one who has answered the questions of a thousand inquisitive guests.

"The name is *malihini*. It's the old Hawaiian word for 'stranger.' I am the exact opposite — a *kamaaina*. I have been born and brought up on the islands. I've played with the natives here ever since I could walk. But what are you doing to amuse yourself tonight?"

"I am going to the Hitchings Plantation," said Wilson. He looked carefully at the man opposite him

64

and realized that the manager had known it all the while. "I wonder if you'd tell me something I am curious about," Wilson continued. "If you've been here always, you must have known a distant cousin of mine — of my father's: Ned Hitchings."

"Ned Hitchings?" the other said, and his formality left him when he said it as though something in the name made him warm and friendly. "Yes, I knew Ned. There aren't many left like him. You should have seen the Plantation in the old days when Ned was playing host. It was a grand place then — music all the time, and all the champagne you could drink. Everybody in the world was there. Nearly any night. Ned was the greatest host in the world. You should have heard his stories! The Hawaiians loved him, everyone in the world loved Ned. There was a time when the old Queen wanted him in her court, but that was long ago."

Wilson was thinking of the former owner when he saw Hitchings Plantation again that night. That mysterious soft darkness of the tropics, which had fallen so suddenly like the dropping of the curtain, had shut out the loneliness of the valley, leaving only the brightness of the house lights shining through the dark. Looking backward far below him, Wilson Hitchings could see the lights of the city like the embers of a huge campfire in the night. The lights of the house where he was going looked like the sparks which had been blown from the edges of that fire.

Now that it was dark an electric light burned above the sign at the gatepost showing the name Hitchings Plantation with a clarity that made him wince; but even so, even as his car moved up the drive, he seemed to feel something of the personality of the man who had made the place. He recalled the words he had heard earlier that evening: "You should have seen the Plantation in the old days when Ned was playing host." There was still an air of genial expansiveness now that it was dark. Although the place was being run for money now, and filled with paying guests, there was still an atmosphere of hospitality, almost of careless generosity, as though money did not matter. The great veranda and the columns spoke of it and so did the wide hall inside. There was no doubt that Ned Hitchings had once lived high. As Wilson walked up the steps he could hear music and laughter and through the window he had a glimpse of people dancing in the hall. There was a man at the door, enormously muscular, a Polynesian with grizzled hair, dressed in white trousers and a white silk shirt, a wreath of flowers around his neck. His features in the glow of light were regular and almost imposing, and Wilson could

66

imagine that he had been with the Plantation for a long while.

"Your card, please, sir," the doorman said, and he read the card carefully, and then he smiled benignly.

"Good evening, sir," he said. "Miss Eva said you might be coming."

"She knew I was coming?" Wilson asked.

"Oh, yes," the doorman smiled again. "Oh, yes, she knew." Wilson smiled back at him as they stood there in the doorway. The hall was brilliantly lighted. There were chairs and tables around the walls such as might have belonged in a gentleman's drawing room, and been moved aside for an informal party. There was a white-shirted orchestra playing stringed instruments in the corner, just as though they had been called in only for the evening, and almost opposite him, in direct line with the door, was an open fireplace, a needless addition to a house in such a climate. Above it was a portrait, three-quarters length, of an elderly man in white, a pleasure-loving man, whose face in the bright light stared out genially over the strangers in the hall. There was no doubt at whom Wilson was looking, for it was a family face, although the countenance was less practical and less austere than the Hitchings faces which Wilson had known. Ned Hitchings in his portrait was looking over his domain, much as he must have done in life. You could see that he would have loved the music and the dancing and the general disorder of the place. Wilson Hitchings smiled at the huge doorman.

"It's a nice house," he said, and the doorman smiled back.

"Yes," he said, "it's a nice house. Everybody has a good time here." He paused and looked about the hall. "Everybody has always had a good time here." Wilson could agree with him. There was something indefinable about the place — an ineradicable sense of happy days and happy nights. Wilson, himself, could feel it.

"Have you got time to show me around?" he asked.

"Oh, yes," the doorman said. "Miss Eva, she wants to see you. Give that boy your hat and come this way."

"Have you been here long?" Wilson asked.

"Oh, yes," the doorman said. "I have worked for Mr. Hitchings always. My family, they have lived here always. They have lived here when Mr. Hitchings bought the land." In a certain way his voice seemed like the Hawaiian music — it had the same sad gaiety.

"Yes, the house is very fine. Miss Eva, she keeps it very well. There is always dancing in the hall and refreshments in the dining room and tables on the great *lanai,* and lights in the garden. Then here are the card rooms and the fan-tan room, and in back the roulette room. Miss Eva will be there."

The music followed them as they walked through room after room on the lower floor of that large house. Except for certain people in the rooms, they might have been in a gentleman's house at an evening party. The house was furnished in excellent taste; the bridge room had been the library and the books were still along the wall. There was a studious concentration in the room, although it did not come from the volumes. The dining room and the great terrace beyond it were set and ready for an evening party.

"You may help yourself to anything you want," the Hawaiian said. "Miss Eva, she won't take no money. The entertainment is on the house. Will you have a glass of wine before you go to the roulette room?"

"Thank you, no," Wilson said.

Wilson was listening to the music and looking at the people. The house was full of people, and he doubted if there would have been such a wholly democratic company in old Ned Hitchings' time. There was one thing they had in common — the guests seemed well-to-do. But beyond this all resemblance ended, because Hitchings Plantation appeared to be open to every type and to every race.

There were tourists easily distinguished from the rest, there were adventurers and adventuresses such as he had seen in other seaports, there were steamship officers, businessmen, and army men in civilian clothing, there were Portuguese, and dusky-skinned part Hawaiians in whose blood ran either white or Chinese strain. It seemed to Wilson that all the visitors who had ever touched the shores had sent some representatives to the racial congress moving through the rooms of Hitchings Plantation. There were Japanese businessmen and bland Chinese and there was a Hindu with his turban — taken altogether they made a mysterious and diverting sight and one which appealed to the imagination. He had read of the varied races on the Hawaiian Islands and of the experiments in Democracy and now he could see it working beneath the protection of the outlawed democracy of chance. There was no apparent prejudice in that mingling of the races. There was nothing but good humor and an order which was almost decorous. It amazed Wilson to find himself thinking that representatives of his own race seemed the least attractive of any in that room, but this may have been because he understood them better. He had seen enough of the world to recognize the political, professional gambler type among his own people and he observed that several men of this sort were watching him curiously and he could imagine what they were thinking. They were thinking of how to reach him and of how to get his money. Still smiling, Wilson turned toward the huge Hawaiian who stood beside him.

"This is all new to me," Wilson said. "Are there always so many different sorts of people here?"

The man's teeth flashed again as he answered.

"Oh, yes, we have all sorts of people on the Island. All people get on very well together on the Island, they have always. So many strangers are surprised like you. Anyone can come here as long as he behaves."

"What if he doesn't behave?" Wilson asked.

The large dark man frowned thoughtfully.

"He is sent away," he said. "There are men to take care of every room. There is never any trouble." The music was playing again, one of those gay sad tunes, and the room was sweet and fresh from the warm air which came through the open doors and windows. He could see lights from the exotic trees on the terrace.

"Miss Hitchings runs this very well," he said. "She must be very capable."

"Oh, yes," the man said. "Miss Eva, she is a fine lady, everybody likes her very much."

"Yes," said Wilson, "so I've heard."

He was glancing toward the door which led to the entrance hall as he said it and he remembered afterwards that he was thinking of the strangeness of the place. He was thinking as he had at first that it had an air of kindly, tolerant hospitality more than any atmosphere of vice or folly. The rooms with their white woodwork were fine and well-proportioned — in spite of everything it was a gentleman's house.

"Well," he said, "shall we go to the roulette room? I mustn't take too much of your time." And then he stopped — a figure in the dining room stopped him, and he felt the same surprise as though someone had called his name. A small man in impeccable evening clothes was standing in the doorway, glancing about the dining room, holding an ivory cigarette holder between two slender delicate fingers. He was examining the room thoughtfully and the light fell on his face.

For an instant Wilson was looking at him straight in the face; for an instant Wilson could not believe it was so, but he had an accurate memory for faces and he knew that face. It was that of the Mr. Moto he had seen in Shanghai, and though it seemed contrary to every possibility, he could have sworn it was Mr. Moto in the doorway.

"Wait a minute, please," said Wilson, and he took a step forward, but as he did so, the small man in the dinner coat turned and walked away and Wilson did not follow him. He suddenly realized that he was being foolish, that there must be a large number of other members of the Japanese race who might resemble Mr. Moto. It occurred to him that he was a long way from any place where Mr. Moto could possibly be.

"Excuse me," Wilson said, "I thought I saw a man I knew, a Japanese I met once in Shanghai, but I must have been mistaken. But Japanese look so much alike."

He was surprised to find the heavy man beside him looking at him curiously. And there was something in the glance which Wilson could not understand. There was no subtlety in that broad dark face. The doorkeeper of Hitchings Plantation looked troubled.

"Yes," the big man said, "Japanese do look very much alike. I think we had better go to find Miss Eva now."

CHAPTER IV

THE roulette room was in what had probably been the owner's study. Like all the other rooms in that strange house it was large and well-proportioned and retained a certain dignity. It was finished in some dark wood — from the Island *ohia* tree, Wilson found out later — with cupboards in the paneling and with high windows opening on another terrace. At one end of the room was a closed door bearing a legend on a brass plaque: DIRECTORS' ROOM, PRIVATE.

The table with its wheel in the middle of that room was a new and an expensive specimen. It gave the place the same atmosphere which a gaming table gives any room no matter on what end of the earth one may find it. Wilson had been in Monte Carlo once. He remembered the faces of the people who had sat or stood about the green baize tables there. They had represented nearly all the nations of Europe or the Near East, from blue-eyed blondes of Scandinavia to olive-tinted Levantines. The tables at Monte Carlo had each reminded him of an amusing parody of the League of Nations, and the table there at Hitchings Plantation was much the same. The cashier, a pale, sharp-eyed man, sat behind the desk near the door through which he entered. There must have been fifteen persons in the room putting counters on the number and watching the turning of the wheel. A third of them were women and the rest were men, again a congress of nations. Some Europeans, some Eurasians, two Chinese in evening clothes, two Japanese, a young American army or navy officer, a red-fisted Norwegian sea captain, a Russian, and again some tourists, those representatives of some world cruise who crop up perpetually in every Pacific port. The croupier was spinning the wheel as Wilson entered, and oddly enough he was speaking in French — the French of Indo-China.

"Faites vos jeux, messieurs, 'dames. . . . Rien ne va plus." The words sounded strangely above the whir and the rattle of the ball in the otherwise silent room — so strangely that the croupier caught Wilson's attention first, making him wonder what strange chance had brought him to the Islands, for like all croupiers he was an interesting man. He seemed to be part French and part Malay, exotic, muscular, and adroit; the swiftness and the accuracy of his eyes were in his fingers. His jaw was square, almost pugnacious; his manners, like all men in his profession, were impeccable. Another man sat

75

beside him whom Wilson imagined was also an employee of the house — a thin, pale man, with an Adam's apple and watery, sleepy eyes that were riveted on the patrons at the table. He looked up as Wilson entered. Their glances met and immediately he looked away, but in that second there was something startling in those watery eyes, something that was icily cold, unhealthy and deliberate, something which told Wilson instinctively that the man was not good company.

The wheel had stopped and the croupier was speaking. *"Rouge impair,"* he said.

There was a decorous clattering of chips and low even voices. A girl in a red silk dress with a pattern of white flowers on it who was seated near the head of the table rose and walked toward them, a tall girl with dark eyes, short wavy auburn hair, and a mouth that was bent upward in a fixed sort of expression of cynical amusement. There was the same amusement in her eyes and an odd sort of nervous vitality which was close to laughter. Her face and her bare arms were brown, she walked toward Wilson with the careless, athletic grace of a dancer, and looked at him squarely.

"Good evening," she was saying.

There was no doubt who she was — she was the head of the house. She had the air of being able to cope with any situation.

"Miss Eva," Wilson's guide said, "this is Mr. Hitchings." Wilson bowed and she nodded to him curtly, but did not hold out her hand.

"Yes," she said; "of course, I've been expecting you. Moku, you may go back to the door now. I'll look after Mr. Hitchings."

Wilson bowed again.

"I'm sure you will," he said, and she nodded in cool agreement.

"Yes," she said, "I'm sure I will. Uncle Joe Wilkie said you were coming. He said you wanted to come incognito, but that was rather silly, wasn't it?"

"Yes," agreed Wilson, "very silly."

"You see," she said, "the Hitchingses are such an important family that everybody knows the name. That's why it's such a help to have it on the house. Shall we go into the directors' room? It will be more quiet there. I suppose you want to talk."

"Thanks," said Wilson, "it might be better. I don't want to disturb your guests."

"I wonder — " she said. "Are you always as considerate as that? This way, please." He followed her toward the door marked PRIVATE, and the croupier was saying, *"Messieurs et mesdames — faites vos jeux!"* — and when the door closed behind them, they were in a smaller room, with bare walls and an oval mahogany table, with Chippendale chairs

77

around it, and windows that looked out into breezy, rustling darkness.

Wilson looked about the room courteously and noticed that there was a second door marked OFFICE. That distant relative of his seated herself at the head of the table.

"Well," she said, "sit down, Mr. Wilson Hitchings, anywhere at all. And if I don't seem polite, it's only because I'm surprised. Few of the family have ever called on us; none, as far as I remember."

"I'm sorry for that," said Wilson, and he sat down in the chair beside her. Her lips curled up but her eyes were cool and unfriendly.

"Well," she said, "on the whole I don't think I'm sorry, because I dislike you all very much." They looked at each other for a moment without speaking, and Wilson tried to imagine what sort of girl she was, and he found it difficult because he had never seen anyone just like her. There was only one thing that he was sure of in that silence which fell between them, and that was that she did not like the Hitchingses. There was something deep, almost venomous in her dislike.

"Would you mind telling me why you don't like us?" he inquired.

"Not in the least," she said; "but there's something I must ask you first. . . . We've always been hospitable to strangers in this house. My father taught me that. Let me order you something to drink, Mr. Hitchings."

Still looking at her, Wilson shook his head.

"No," he said, "thank you just as much."

"I suppose," she replied, and her tone was acidly polite, "that you don't want anything to disturb your logic. The Hitchings were always so cold-blooded."

"No," said Wilson, "it isn't that. I've always made it a rule only to drink with friends, that's all. Why is it you don't like us, Miss Hitchings? It might help if I could find that out."

Her hands were lying on the table and they closed and opened as he spoke and her lips were pressed together more tightly. For the first time it occurred to Wilson that the girl beside him had a temper and that she was having difficulty in maintaining her cool poise. He could see a glint of anger in her eyes which made him add another statement quite deliberately.

"When I am sitting with a pretty girl," he said, "I don't need to drink. You are fortunate that you don't resemble the Hitchingses. You don't resemble us at all."

She leaned toward him and there was a catch in her voice as she answered.

"That's the nicest thing you could possibly say. It makes me feel better than I have for a long while. Thank Heaven! I don't resemble them at all."

"Yes, it is a relief," said Wilson easily. "I was afraid you would have our nose, and that's a drawback. You have got our jaw, though, and that is your very worst feature — a stubborn jaw. Do you mind if I smoke?"

"Don't be foolish," she said, "I don't mind anything you do."

"That makes everything easier," said Wilson, and he took out a cigarette case and laid it on the table. "And, of course, you won't mind anything I say, either?"

"No," she answered, "not a bit. Why should I?" Wilson pushed the cigarette case toward her and she shook her head.

"Then you won't mind if I say that I like you," he said. "I like you so much that I haven't the slightest intention of saying anything or of doing anything that may offend you. You know why I am here, I suppose? I may as well come to the point." He smiled and lighted his cigarette. "I like this place so much that I'd like to buy it. Can you think of me as a stranger who is making you a business proposal? That might be the easiest way for everyone."

She raised her head a trifle and that flicker of amusement which he had observed the first moment that he saw her came over her face again reminding him of wind rippling over placid water. He could believe that she was pleased that he asked the question and that the whole moment pleased her. Her smile grew more pronounced as she sat there considering his suggestion and the smile took away some of the hardness from her face, making her look younger and less experienced. It made Wilson realize that she was younger than he was. It made him think for the first time that she might be an agreeable person under agreeable circumstances. For the first time he realized that there was a warmth and a charm in Eva Hitchings. In some way, without his being able to explain why, she had ceased to be an abstraction, a purely business problem, and had become an attractive girl who did not belong in that environment. She even appealed to his protective instinct, although he put the thought away from him at once. He examined her more attentively; she had none of the attributes of a hostess at a gambling house, her red and white dress was simple and in perfect taste, and her color was natural and she wore no jewelry. Her hands, as they lay before her on the table, were beautiful. They were a lady's hands, sensitive, indicative of breeding. He suddenly suspected that her hardness and her control were purely make-believe. More the product of a strong will than character.

"Well," she asked him, "suppose you begin by telling me why do you want to buy my house? Do you want to run it, Mr. Hitchings?"

"I wonder why you ask me," Wilson inquired, "when you know the reasons very well already."

"Because I want to hear you give those reasons," she answered. "You can, can't you?"

If Wilson had never believed that there was something in inheritance he would have believed it then, because he was almost surprised at the clarity and the order of his thoughts. Now that he sat there at the table he knew that he had the family ability for negotiation and for estimating a situation. All the details, all the things that he had seen and heard, came accurately together in his mind by a curious sort of instinct. His mind moved easily toward a number of truths, even while he was speaking.

"Please don't forget that I'm not here for myself," he said. "I was sent here by the family. I rather like this place. Personally I rather admire you for running it, because it can't be such a pleasant thing for you to do. It must take a great deal of experience and a great deal of ability. And I don't believe you like it very much, do you, Miss Hitchings? I don't believe you like being cordial to all the riffraff I've seen in this house to-night. It can't be pleasant to combine hospitality with business. It made me think you'd be a different sort of person, and I see you're not. You can't like that croupier of yours, and that man behind him, very much."

Eva Hitchings shrugged her shoulders.

"Don't preach," she said. "I asked you why you wanted to buy this place."

"I'm not preaching," Wilson answered. "As a matter of fact I think you're a rather brave girl to be doing this. I wish you could think that I was speaking to you as a member of our family, however distant. I don't like to think of any of our family having to be in your position. I really think, although no one has said so, that that is what disturbs my father and my uncle more than anything else."

"Oh," said Eva Hitchings. "You mean it rather shocks you?"

"No," said Wilson, "I know you'd like to have it shock me, but it doesn't. Nothing shocks me very much, because we're living in a rather shock-proof time. I know plenty of girls at home running teashops and working in department stores. There's nothing you could do that could shock me because you're not the kind."

"Really?" said Eva Hitchings. "You might be very much surprised."

"I doubt it," said Wilson. "I doubt it very much. But of course there's another aspect which you know as well as I do. Our name on your house is not good for a banking business. Then there's a second reason why I'm here to buy your house. It's a beautiful place, and of course you must be fond of it. I don't want to speak too much about money because you're in the family, but I'd like to have you live in this house as you'd like to live. How would it be if you still owned it and took the sign off the gate? And had it as a place for your own friends the way it used to be? Would you like that, Miss Hitchings?"

"Well," she said, "go on, what else?"

"If you agree," Wilson added, "we will talk about a sum in trust, the income of which will keep you comfortably. Things can't go on like this, you must see that."

Eva Hitchings leaned toward him. "Why not?" she asked.

Wilson lowered his voice and spoke more slowly.

"Because sooner or later you'll get into trouble," he said. "As a matter of fact, I think you're in trouble now."

He could tell that she was startled when he said it, more from instinct than from any change in her. She was smiling but her eyes were wider.

"Why do you think that?" she asked. Although her voice was level and pleasant he knew that she was startled. He could feel it in the room and in the rustling of the wind outside.

"Do you really want me to tell you why?" he asked.

"Yes," she said. Her voice was too casual, too easy. "I shall be delighted, Mr. Hitchings." Wilson took a paper from his pocket — it was the typewritten sheet which he had found in the room of his hotel.

"Read it," he said. "I wonder who sent me this? I don't think you are the kind of person who would do it. You're not as stupid as all that."

He watched her as she read the paper and he had to admire her composure. She read it and she laughed. It was the first time he had heard her laugh — her laughter was easy and pleasant and there was a ring of intimacy in it which seemed to bring them nearer together.

"You're right," she said. "I'm not such a fool as that."

"And now," said Wilson, "I'll tell you what I think. You needn't tell me if I'm right or wrong. You're not running this place all yourself, Miss Hitchings! You're not the kind to do it. You have some people running it for you. I have watched everything outside; everything is smooth and very professional, as professional as a New York night club. You're the front, Miss Hitchings, but there is someone else behind you. Whoever that may be, and I don't care who it is, because it's none of my business, is afraid that you may sell out. Whoever it may be is trying to stop you; that's why I got this note. And that's exactly why I think you'd better sell out.

85

There's nothing for you to gain by not selling."
There was a silence when he had finished. He could hear the sound of music and the sound of the trade wind, and she was looking at him as other people had looked at him sometimes — half surprised, almost with respect.

"You're rather clever, aren't you, Mr. Hitchings?" she said. "I didn't know you could be so clever with your environment and background!"

Wilson nodded. Her eyes and her voice were almost friendly, and it was as though they were playing some sort of a game, and he rather enjoyed the game because there were so many imponderables in it and because he and she were alone togther. Some barrier between them had dropped down after he had spoken and he found himself telling her exactly what he thought.

"You know I'm a little surprised at myself," he said; "because all this is new to me; this is the first time I've ever been entirely on my own. I suppose I may be clever, as you say. I never thought of it exactly that way before, but it suddenly came over me, now that I have seen you and now that I have talked to you, that you are in trouble. After all, we're both in the family. I hope that you'll remember that. I have come here for a definite purpose, but I really hope you'll believe that I want to help you. I thought you'd be quite a different person. I don't like seeing you here alone." She did not answer for a moment. She only sat looking at him, puzzled and seemingly undecided what to say.

"You're different than you look," she said. "You're different than I thought you would be, too. I wonder if you're frank, or if this is just an act. I suppose it's just an act."

"No," said Wilson. "I'm being frank. I've only said exactly what I think. I'm not tricky; actually I'm rather a guileless person."

She sat up straighter, still looking at him, and then she spoke carefully as though she had made up her mind exactly what to say, and he knew that she was saying something which had been on her mind for a long while.

"You'd make a very good gambler, Mr. Hitchings," she said. "I ought to know because I've seen plenty of them in the last few years. I never knew it until just this moment. You have a gambler's face, you have a gambler's coolness; you've played your cards exactly like a professional. I don't believe you are guileless because everything you have said has been so perfectly balanced. You have appealed to me in every possible way and you've really done it very well — so much better than I thought you would. You've been frank, and now it's my turn. And now I'll say my little piece."

"I wish you would," said Wilson.

"You've only made one mistake," she answered. "Your mistake is in talking to me about the family — that was exactly the wrong card to play, because I hate the family. I wonder if I can make you understand how much I hate them. Your family turned on my father because he didn't have your cool face, Mr. Hitchings — and didn't have ice water in his blood; because he wasn't correct and poised like you; because he didn't do the right thing. He made the great mistake of marrying my mother — I'm very glad he did, because that's why I'm not like you, that's why I haven't got your self-importance and your manners, and your easy condescension. That's why I'm a plebeian, Mr. Hitchings. And why I associate with these low people. And I'll tell you something more — Father was not a businessman. When he lost his money, when his back was to the wall, when you could have helped him easily, as you are offering to help me now, not a member of your family raised its hand. You're only doing it now, and you know it, because I'm interfering with your business interests. If you want to know the truth, I had made up my mind to interfere with them, after Father died."

"Simply out of spite?" said Wilson.

"Yes," she answered, "simply out of spite. I am paying you back by running this place. I know I am. And one of the pleasantest moments I have had is

88

to be able to sit here and to tell you so. To see you come here, and to hear you try to buy me out. This place is going to run as long as I can run it and as long as it can hurt the Hitchingses. You couldn't buy it for a million dollars! Is that quite clear?"

"Yes," said Wilson, "it's very clear; but it's rather foolish, don't you think?"

"No," she answered, "not if you knew what I've been through on account of the Hitchings family; it's not foolish to me at any rate. I hate every one of you — I hate your sanctimonious pretence."

"Do you hate me?" Wilson asked.

"Yes," she said, "of course I hate you. And I have sat here long enough, listening to your patronage. I'd like to see you try to close this place! I'd like to see any of you try."

"Well," said Wilson, "I'm sorry. At any rate, I don't want to see it closed to-night; I rather like it."

"Then go out and enjoy yourself," Miss Hitchings said, "we've been here long enough." Wilson rose.

"It's been good of you to give me so much time," he said. "I think I'll try roulette."

"Don't mention it," said Miss Hitchings, "the pleasure has been all mine. I hope you will have a pleasant evening."

"You are sure you don't want to be friends?" said Wilson.

"No," said Miss Hitchings, "I'm sure I don't."

There was a discreet tapping on the door and a Japanese servant entered. "A gentleman wants to see you, Miss," he said.

"Very well," said Miss Hitchings. "Show him into the office." And she turned to Wilson, smiling. "I'm sorry that I am busy now," she said.

"So am I," said Wilson. "Good evening, Miss Hitchings!" Then, just as he turned away, he found that the other gentleman was entering — Mr. Moto was standing in the doorway, bowing, smiling.

"Excuse me," he was saying, "do I interrupt?"

There was no doubt in Wilson now that it was Mr. Moto.

"No," Miss Hitchings said, "this gentleman is just leaving."

"Yes," said Wilson, "I'm leaving." He hoped that he showed no surprise, he hoped that he was smiling as cordially as Mr. Moto.

"Good evening, Mr. Moto," he said. "I thought I saw you a while ago. I did not think I'd see you here."

"Oh, yes," said Mr. Moto, "isn't it very nice? Such a nice place, so beautiful. How nice to see you, Mr. Hitchings." And Mr. Moto drew in his breath through his shining gold teeth.

It sometimes seemed strange to Wilson how small half-forgotten details returned to him later when he reconstructed that scene. All sorts of things registered in his memory — the black rectangles of the open windows, the sound of the wind outside as it rustled through large unfamiliar leaves, the scratches on that bare oval table where the light struck it, the shine of the light in Eva Hitchings' close-cropped hair, that half malicious, half mischievous smile of hers because she was composed again, completely herself. There had been a moment in that outburst of her anger when she had revealed a new side of her personality. He had been able to understand her loyalty and her bitterness, not so much by what she had said as by its implication. There must have been some prepossessing quality about Ned Hitchings, for his daughter had loved him as everyone else seemed to have who had known him, in spite of all his faults.

But what surprised Wilson most was the unexpected interest which she had aroused in him, which was more than curiosity. She had not spoken of her loneliness but he had seen it. She was not a person who was meant to be alone. Suddenly he realized that he was thinking of her emotionally, not logically; that she was appealing indirectly to his sense of chivalry, and he knew that this was foolish. Then he heard Mr. Moto speaking again.

"Please," Mr. Moto was saying, "I'm afraid I interrupt."

That close-clipped voice of Mr. Moto's brought

him to himself and made him realize that both of those persons in the room were waiting for him to go and that he had been standing almost stupidly with his hand on the knob of the door looking at Eva Hitchings.

"I'm sorry," he said. "Good night."

"Good night," said Eva Hitchings.

He remembered that Mr. Moto had been glancing at the open window as he spoke.

"Good night," said Mr. Moto. "I shall see you soon again, I hope. It will be so very nice."

Eva Hitchings was standing motionless waiting for him to go and Mr. Moto was glancing back at the windows. Wilson's back was half turned, he was reaching for the doorknob, when a sound like the snap of a whip made him whirl about. Even with his back to the room, he knew that the sound had come from the night outside. It was its sharpness more than its loudness which startled him. His first thought as he was turning was that a motor had back-fired in the driveway, and in the same second he was ashamed that he had started.

"I am sorry," he began, "I didn't mean to jump." And then he stopped. He found himself looking at Mr. Moto. Something had happened in that instant which was very odd. Mr. Moto was crouching, staring out of an open window. He was holding a small automatic pistol, he was absolutely motionless, evidently listening. In that first second of amazement Wilson did not move. He remembered that he glanced almost stupidly about the room wondering what had happened, for nothing in the room had changed. Eva Hitchings was standing just as he had seen her last but she was no longer smiling. She was holding tight to the back of the chair, also staring at the open window.

"What's the matter?" said Wilson. "What was that?"

No one answered for the moment. Mr. Moto still peered into the darkness and Eva Hitchings gave no sign of hearing. Then, still holding his pistol, Mr. Moto straightened himself and turned away from the window. It seemed to Wilson that his color was lighter, but Mr. Moto was smiling. And his eyes were dark and placid.

"Excuse me," he said, "I think perhaps you know. It was a pistol shot — the bullets will be in the wall somewhere behind me. The man was a very bad marksman, Miss Hitchings. You should get one who is more steady. Yes, he was very bad and I was very very foolish. I did not think that such a thing would happen. Yes, I was very very foolish, but I do not think that he will try again to-night because he moved away. The next time that you and Mr. Hitchings try to kill me, will you do it better, please. I hope you will. Thank you very very much. And now, Mr. Hitchings, please stand away from the door. I think I shall be going now. Good evening, Miss Hitchings! Thank you very very much."

There had not been much excitement in Wilson Hitchings' life and the idea of such a piece of melodrama was more than he could grasp at once. The thing had happened so suddenly, and yet so casually, that it became ordinary and matter of fact. The ordinary quality of such an episode seemed reflected in Mr. Moto's manner, and judging from appearances such an event had happened often in Mr. Moto's life.

"What do you mean?" said Wilson, and he still stood in front of the door. His sense of law and order was so outraged that his mind moved dully trying to reconcile what had happened with ordinary fact. "What are you talking about, Mr. Moto?"

He had thought of Mr. Moto in the past as an insignificant man but now he looked as compact and as nerveless and as efficient as the pistol he was carrying. Mr. Moto's dinner coat was double-breasted and cut in extreme lines; his round head and his black hair arranged in a shoebrush pattern was almost grotesque, but there was nothing grotesque about Mr. Moto's answer.

"Excuse me, please, if I did not make myself clear," he said, "perhaps I was excited. Please, I am not excited now." Mr. Moto's eyes were bright and steady, he was breathing fast through his closed teeth. "A shot was fired at me through the open window. I'm very very sorry — I did not expect one so soon. Attempts have been made to liquidate me before, Mr. Hitchings. Enough of them so that I should have been more careful. I had not thought I had been asked to this room to be murdered. I am very very much surprised. Please, I shall be going now." And he took a step toward Wilson, who stood with his back to the door.

Wilson glanced at Eva Hitchings. The girl looked pale and frightened but she did not speak, and the absurdity of the situation began to dawn on him. Mr. Moto and his automatic looked absurd, so amusing all at once that he almost smiled.

"Well," said Wilson, "I've always heard you Japanese were egotists. Do you really think I paid a man to stand outside to murder you, Mr. Moto?"

Mr. Moto smiled.

"Excuse me," he said, "I'm so very very sorry. It is not nice to say so, but I think that is what you and Miss Hitchings did. Excuse me, I must be careful. Please do not move your hands."

"And what do you propose to do about it?" Wilson asked. He found the matter increasingly amusing. The idea of his being connected with Eva Hitchings in any capacity amused him.

"I propose to do nothing about it," said Mr. Moto.

And he said it genially, like someone anxious to be kind and forgiving. "These matters happen, do they not? Let us say no more about it, please. It would be very very much better, don't you think? Please, it does not make me angry. It was so very badly done."

"Perhaps you won't mind then," suggested Wilson, "if I tell you what I think."

"Oh, no," said Mr. Moto, "except I am in a hurry to be going, please."

Wilson moved a step nearer to him and looked down at Mr. Moto.

"Please," said Mr. Moto again, "do not move your hands."

Then Wilson heard Eva Hitchings speak and her voice sounded frightened.

"Don't," she said softly, "don't move."

Wilson thrust his hands deliberately into the side pockets of his coat.

"That will do for your giving me orders, Mr. Moto," he said pleasantly, "personally I think you are rather too high-strung, and that you have a powerful imagination. I don't know much about these things but I don't believe anybody fired at you, Mr. Moto. Try to think of it calmly; a car made a noise outside probably. Or else a window shade snapped up. Now, if I were you I'd put that pistol in your pocket where it won't do any harm. I don't know what manners are in Japan but I don't think you have been very polite to Miss Hitchings, Mr. Moto, and you have startled her a good deal. Personally, I don't mind; in fact, I rather enjoy it, but I think it would be very very nice if you said 'good night' to Miss Hitchings and begged her pardon."

Mr. Moto's expression had changed since Wilson had spoken; his forehead had wrinkled into little creases; he looked puzzled, almost hurt.

"Excuse me," he said, "I do not understand. Please, do you think this is funny, Mr. Hitchings?"

"Yes," said Wilson, "mildly funny. Now don't you think you'd better put that gun away? And tell Miss Hitchings you are sorry? I won't hurt you, Mr. Moto, really I won't."

Mr. Moto put his pistol in his pocket and his breath hissed through teeth, then his tenseness and his watchfulness entirely disappeared, and he bowed his head to Eva Hitchings. There was a strange, submissive dignity in his bow.

"Excuse me, please," he said, "if I have done anything to be rude. I am so very very sorry, and I am so very very sorry if I have been funny. Excuse me, please. Good evening, please."

Wilson opened the door to the roulette room and when he closed it he began to laugh.

"Excuse me, please," said he to Eva Hitchings. "I am very very sorry." Then something on the dark

97

polished floor, near the wall, caught his attention, he never knew just why. Close by the door he had just shut were a few grains of new white plaster. Something made him look upward to the wall. There was a small hole where something had struck and had knocked the plaster down. He looked from the dent in the wall toward Eva Hitchings, curiously. She was no longer the same person he had seen before — she had regained her poise, but she was no longer as she had been before Moto had come in. Somehow as she stood there, resting her hands on the back of the chair, she looked enigmatic and extremely capable.

There was a mysterious quality about that dent in the wall which changed the point of view. Wilson could feel a number of illusions leaving him and the sensation was almost physical. For one thing he felt as cold as though he had lost a comfortable covering; for another his visual faculties seemed entirely different. Eva Hitchings was no longer a lonely girl, no longer a flower on a midden, not to be associated with such a place as Hitchings Plantation. She was looking at him coolly, almost contemptuously, he thought, and in a way which made his next remark seem immature and stupid.

"So it was a shot?" he said.

Her shining reddish head moved in a brief sarcastic nod.

"What did you think it was?" she inquired, "a bean from a blower? This isn't exactly a Sunday School, Mr. Hitchings."

Wilson leaned against the wall with his hands in his pockets watching her. He did not know what attracted him, certainly nothing which was right. He knew that he was close to something which was dangerous and he had never known that danger would carry with it an intriguing fascination. He was aware of a strange exaltation beneath his training of habit and formality.

"You're quite right," he agreed. "This isn't like any Sunday School that I remember. And you're not like a Sunday School teacher, either."

"No, but I could teach you a good deal," she said. "I could teach you enough so that your family wouldn't know you, Mr. Hitchings! Perhaps you have learned already that this isn't the place for you. The name of Hitchings is being dragged in the mud, isn't it?" She paused and laughed and seated herself on the edge of the table, and Wilson noticed mechanically that she wore gold slippers, and that her legs were bare. "I hoped for a minute that you were going to be dragged in the mud, too. It did look as though you were going to get into a brawl with Mr. Moto — that wouldn't have looked well, would it? A Hitchings shot at Hitchings Plantation? That would have made the family jump."

He could not understand why the remark annoyed him as much as it did.

"I should have been careful of him," he said. "I don't want to hurt any of your friends." She laughed again and swung her slippers slowly back and forth, tossing her head back a little, and holding to the edge of the table.

"Don't be so naïve," she said, "and don't worry. I'll see you won't get hurt."

"Thank you," said Wilson. "I suppose you know who fired that shot?"

Her face had grown hard again; she looked at him without speaking for a moment.

"If I were you," she said, "I'd keep my lily white hands out of this, because it's none of your business, Mr. Hitchings."

"I wonder," said Wilson. "It might be my business if that shot were meant for me; perhaps you know whom it was meant for — me or Mr. Moto. Would it be too forward of me if I asked you?"

The gold slippers were motionless; she leaned toward him and her eyes grew narrow.

"What do you mean by that?" she asked.

"I mean," said Wilson, "that you are not exactly a Sunday School teacher, Cousin Eva. You can't help my having vague ideas."

Her voice changed; it was low and urgent.

"Stop! Be quiet," she said.

Wilson Hitchings smiled at her, he could not understand why he felt so tolerant or so kindly toward her unless it was because of a sense of his own superiority. He thought his remark had frightened and shocked her; certainly she looked frightened.

"Why should I be quiet, Cousin Eva?" he asked. "Have you got a sense of free guilt, as the psychologists put it?" Then her expression told him that she was not listening, at least not to him. He saw that she was tense and motionless, staring at something beyond his right shoulder and he turned and followed her glance. The door to the roulette room was opening very slowly.

"What is it?" asked Eva Hitchings. "Who is that?"

It was the man with the watery eyes, the watcher at the roulette table. Now that Wilson saw him standing up, the man's awkwardness was gone. The man was thin with a whiplike thinness and his voice showed he was a long way from home. It was a New York City voice.

"It's me, ain't it," he said. He spoke slowly, huskily, as he closed the door behind him and walked almost noiselessly to the center of the room. "I thought maybe there might be a little argument in here." He looked Wilson slowly up and down. "Who's the guy, Miss Eva?"

Miss Eva slid down from the table.

"Have I, or have I not told you not to interrupt me, Paul?" she asked. "You might frighten someone sneaking in that way."

"Nuts!" the thin man said softly. "Who's the guy?"

"This is Mr. Hitchings," Miss Eva said. "This is Mr. Maddock," Miss Eva said.

Mr. Maddock's pale eyes turned upon Wilson unblinkingly; his Adam's apple moved languidly.

"Oh, it's you, is it?" he said. "How are you, pal?"

Wilson Hitchings stared back at him. There had been a sneering lightness in his speech which was entirely new to him, and Mr. Maddock represented a world he had never known, but Wilson knew enough to know it was not a congenial world.

"Quite well," he said, "under the circumstances."

"Oh, yeah!" said Mr. Maddock. "Well, this is a funny place, pal."

"Yes," said Wilson, "and there are lots of funny people in it."

Mr. Maddock's thin lips formed themselves into a smile.

"You got that wrong," he said softly. "I'm not so funny, pal. Has this boy been getting fresh, Miss Eva? I thought there was some trouble here."

"I wish you'd mind your own business," said Eva Hitchings shortly. "Mr. Hitchings and I have been talking — why should you think there has been any trouble?" A lump in Mr. Maddock's throat moved slowly and he glanced casually toward the open window.

"I'm funny that way," he said in that soft voice of his. "I always did have a sense for trouble, see? That's what makes me useful, see? I seen that Japanese come out of here and I did not like his looks. He looked like someone had tried to run him out and then when no one else came after him — " Mr. Maddock paused and shrugged his shoulders. "You know how things happen among customers; we've got to watch everything, Miss Eva."

"Well, nothing happened," Miss Eva said.

Mr. Maddock walked toward her softly; his pale face looked cynical and kindly.

"Listen, girlie," he said, "it couldn't be that Hitchings came here to make you a proposition? You wouldn't be holding out on me, would you?"

"No," said Eva Hitchings promptly, "of course I wouldn't, Paul. Mr. Hitchings has come here to buy me out and I've turned him down."

Mr. Maddock took a long thin cigar from his inside pocket and lighted it very carefully.

"That's the little lady," he said softly, then he turned to Wilson and exhaled a cloud of smoke. "Tough luck," he said, "but she knows who her friends are, pal."

"Yes," said Wilson, "I'm sure she does." Mr. Maddock removed his cigar from the corner of his mouth.

"It's getting kind of late, pal," he suggested. "Maybe you had better be going home."

"Why," asked Wilson, "do you own this place? I'm not in any hurry to go." Then he heard Eva Hitchings laugh, and she spoke before Mr. Maddock could answer.

"Paul," she said, "will you send someone to bring around my car? Mr. Hitchings was just leaving. I am going to drive him home."

"Drive me home?" echoed Wilson, and he tried not to show his surprise. "You don't have to — but it's very kind."

"It will be better for you if I did, I think," Eva Hitchings answered, and Mr. Maddock raised his eyebrows.

"What's the big idea?" Mr. Maddock asked. "Some of the boys can take him."

Eva Hitchings shook her head. "No," she said, "I'd like the ride." Mr. Maddock frowned thoughtfully.

"You're lucky, pal," he said, "it isn't everybody who gets a ride with her."

"Yes," said Wilson politely, "I'm sure I'm very lucky."

"Well," said Mr. Maddock, "I'll be seeing you."

CHAPTER V

WILSON followed Eva into the dark-paneled room where the roulette game was going decorously forward beneath that indefinable shadow of concentration which always hovers above a well-conducted gaming table. There was no sound but the whirring of the wheel and the rattle of the ball moving distractedly in its first burst of speed. No one looked up as they entered. They might have been walking into a laboratory where scientists were gathered to watch a final, critical experiment, and yet Wilson Hitchings had never felt so strangely, so mysteriously alive. All his senses seemed to have awakened into a peculiar stimulated watchfulness. He had never felt so much like an actor in a play. He was aware almost unconsciously of mysterious, possibly of dangerous matters, all around him. He was aware that anything might happen. But he was surprised to find that the knowledge stimulated rather than disturbed him.

Miss Eva Hitchings walked in front of him carelessly, gracefully; and he remembered thinking that everything tended to make her desirably beautiful, just as though he and she were characters in a romantic story. Mr. Maddock was walking just behind him. He could feel Mr. Maddock's presence and he knew that it was dangerous. Even so, the sight of the table interested him. The imponderables of the laws of chance were calling to something in his blood. It may have been that those imponderables were a good deal like the unknown factors around him, and a good deal like life. He knew that you could not beat life any more than you could beat the house, and it struck him that the thought was interesting, although he knew that it was rather cheap and trite. He could not beat life any more than Eva Hitchings or Mr. Moto, or the slender Mr. Maddock. They were all together in some pattern, according to some logic of chance, like the numbers in the squares. The lights and the green of the table were making him speak almost before he thought. They almost made him forget his immediate problems.

"Do you mind if I play for a few moments?" he asked. "I should like to leave some money with the house."

Eva Hitchings looked at him over her bare, brown shoulder.

"That's what the tables are intended for," she

said. "That is, if you are sure it won't hurt your morals."

"Mr. Maddock will watch my morals," said Wilson. "Won't you, Mr. Maddock?"

"Yes," said Mr. Maddock, softly. "I'll watch your morals, pal. The cashier's desk is over there. The numbers have been running odd to-night around the second dozen, in case you want to know."

"Thank you," said Wilson. "Thank you very much." And he spoke to Eva Hitchings again. "Don't go away. You might bring me luck."

"I am very much in doubt if I'll do that," she said.

"After all," said Wilson, "you never can tell, can you?"

He bought fifty dollars' worth of chips and stood by the table for a minute or two watching. He saw that the play was heavy. A Chinese in evening clothes with a large heap of chips in front of him was playing the numbers covering an area with his bets. Wilson watched him lose once and watched him lose again, all the while his mind was working along channels which were new to him. It was probably the Hitchings instinct to be careful of money which made him wait patiently until he could form some definite plan of action. He watched the imperturbable croupier and the masklike man at the wheel. Judging from the personnel, he believed that the game was probably a crooked one. He could understand that the house at that hour of the evening might be coveting the winnings of its Chinese guest.

Thus logically he knew that it was better to confine his activities to some other section of the board. He had seen the game before and he understood enough of the combinations not to play entirely like a beginner. He bet on *manque* and doubled his stake. He placed it on red and lost. He made a play *à cheval* and lost again. And then he won on a *transversale pleine.* He was playing idly, carelessly, without any thought except to keep away from the region of heavy betting. Then suddenly he had a streak of luck. He played *en carré* and won, increasing his stake eight times. Taking out half of his money, he placed the remainder on the cross between twenty-eight, twenty-nine, thirty-one and thirty-two; and thirty-one came up. His luck was causing a ripple of interest, but the Chinese player across the table from him played placidly, still losing. Then, a few seconds after the wheel was placed in motion, Wilson placed a stake where the zero and three joined *manque,* and won again. He pulled his chips into a pile without bothering to count them, and put the total on black. He was neither surprised nor elated when he won, because he had the sense that winning was the result of some vague sort of justice.

"Well," said Eva Hitchings, "what next?"

"No next," said Wilson and he scooped the chips into his pocket. "Not to-night."

"The Hitchingses are always careful, aren't they?" Eva Hitchings said.

"No," said Wilson, "but sometimes they know when to stop." He did not realize until he had cashed the counters that he had won five hundred dollars. The looks of the croupiers made it very plain that not many guests left the table with such heavy winnings in their pockets, and that he had done a good deal to cut the profits of the evening. He handed a hundred dollars to the two croupiers by the wheel and another hundred to Mr. Maddock.

"Something to remember me by, in case I come back again," he said.

"Thanks," said Mr. Maddock, sourly. "We'll remember you all right."

"I'm sure you will," said Wilson, and then Eva Hitchings was saying, "My car is outside, if you don't want to stay."

They walked together through the innocent-looking front rooms where the only amusements were bridge and supper and dancing. There was a runabout by the front steps, and the doorman, in his white clothes, was standing by the running board. Wilson handed him two bills.

"Excuse me, sir," the man said, "there must be

109

some mistake. You've given me two hundred dollars."

"No," said Wilson. "No mistake at all."

The car jumped forward viciously as Eva Hitchings stamped her foot on the accelerator.

"Why did you throw the money away?" she asked. "On account of religious scruples?"

Wilson Hitchings laughed. He felt extraordinarily gay, irrationally elated, although something told him that he should be careful. Something told him that he knew nothing about the girl beside him; but he did not mind. What interested him more was that she was quite different from anyone he had ever known. As he sat beside her, with his shoulder touching hers, he felt kindly toward her, almost sympathetic.

"I didn't want to take your money," he said.

"Thank you," she answered. "It was a pretty, if a rather vulgar gesture. You can't buy Moku for two hundred dollars. He was on the place before I was born."

"Honestly," said Wilson, "I didn't want to buy him."

"Didn't you?" she answered. "I thought perhaps you did."

"I wish you wouldn't be so suspicious," Wilson said. "I don't mean you any harm."

"Really?" she answered. "Perhaps I am franker

than you are. I mean you a good deal of harm. You might as well know it, Mr. Hitchings."

Wilson did not answer for a moment. They were moving down a dark valley through warm, heavy, mysterious darkness which seemed to shut them away from any particular reality. The headlights of the automobile made dancing circles along the edge of the road revealing strange trees and flowers that flashed up exotically from the black and disappeared as the car moved on.

"I have an idea that you saved me a good deal of trouble by taking me home," he said. "I'm grateful to you for that."

"Don't be grateful," she answered. "I've an idea that you can look out for yourself very well, Mr. Hitchings."

"Then you have a higher opinion of me than I have," he said.

"I hope not," she answered, "because I have a rather low opinion."

"Then why are you taking me home?" he asked. He could not see her face in the dark, but her voice sounded amused and almost friendly.

"Because I have never seen anyone like you."

"Well," said Wilson, "I've never seen anyone like you. Have you always lived here, Miss Hitchings?"

"Yes, Mr. Hitchings," she said. "Always."

"Then you must know the place rather well," said

Wilson. "It all seems rather strange to me. How are you able to run the Plantation? It must be against the law."

"It's a private club," she said. "It's quiet. Why do you ask me? You know how such things are done."

Wilson looked at the road ahead of him. They were moving toward the lights of the city and he could see the sea in front of them, dark against the lighter horizon.

"You shouldn't be doing it," he said. "It's a rotten sort of business." She moved impatiently, and her voice was sharp.

"No rottener than yours," she answered. "You needn't preach to me."

"Would you mind telling me," Wilson asked her, "what you mean by that?"

"That's what I'm here for," she said. "That — and curiosity. I think you might as well know exactly where I stand. I think it would make things much simpler. When we get to your hotel, if you'll walk with me up the beach, I'll tell you. I'm not afraid of you, Mr. Hitchings."

"I'm glad of that," said Wilson. "There's no need for you to be."

"Isn't there?" she asked him. "Excuse me, if I don't agree with you. I've watched you to-night. I know a good deal about people and I think that you're a very able and a very unscrupulous and a very dangerous sort of person. I used to think that Paul Maddock and some of the other boys were dangerous, but they take second place when it comes to you. They haven't got your coolness. They haven't got your poise. They haven't your personality."

Wilson Hitchings wanted to laugh but he did not. The whole affair was as unreal as the place around him.

"Are you serious?" he asked.

"Do you really think I am joking?" she inquired. "There is only one thing that puzzles me. I admire you, in a way. I suppose it is because I have always admired people who do things well and who can take a chance without being nervous. I admired you with Mr. Moto, to-night. I liked the way you placed your bets at the table. You did it in such a well-bred way. I think you would shoot anyone very nicely. You must dance very nicely. You must make love very nicely; but you had better not try with me."

Wilson Hitchings drew in his breath. He was glad that she could not see the astonishment that he must have shown.

"You make me rather surprised about myself," he said. "Now shall I tell you what I think of you?"

"I wish you would," she answered.

"All right," said Wilson. "It's a little difficult, because I'm rather confused. Everything that has happened to-night has rather confused me. I got off the

113

boat this morning, in my opinion, a rather ineffective person. Now I'm a dangerous man. I think you have a very vivid imagination. Now, personally, I've been thinking that you're a dangerous girl, exactly the sort that I've been warned against. The sort of girl who might turn my head and make me forget the serious purposes in life. But perhaps we both are wrong. Shall we let it go at that?"

He heard a laugh in the dark beside him.

"No one could turn your head," she answered, "or else, perhaps, I'd try." She stopped the car. "Here's the beach," she said. "We might walk on it for a while. I can always talk better when I am not driving."

"I'm surprised," said Wilson, "that you're not afraid to be alone with me."

"Yes," she answered. "So am I."

What surprised him most was that her voice was neither entirely sarcastic nor unfriendly. Instead she seemed to have a rather reluctant admiration for him, as though she actually believed what she was saying. Although not a word of it was true, although he had no great vanity, that admiration was curiously comforting. Oddly enough it made him see himself in a different light. It made him come close to believing that he might have certain unsuspected capabilities. At any rate that inaccurate picture which Eva Hitchings had of him was not entirely unpleasant to his imagination. Indeed he often thought afterwards that it had something to do with his subsequent actions, simply because of a desire to make her see that she was not entirely wrong. In some ways that picture of himself blended perfectly with the setting. He had never felt more like an adventurer. He had never before felt carried so far beyond the limits of reason.

The windows of the hotel where he was staying were rectangles of yellow light. The outlines of the building itself were vague against the stars in the sky. They were walking down a path toward the beach through a grove of tall coconut palms. The fronds of the palms clattered in the steady trade wind above their heads like the flapping wings of unseen birds. They made a mild sound when one heard them above the beating of the waves on the coral reef, perhaps a half-mile offshore. And, with that elemental music, there came snatches of a tune from a stringed orchestra which told him that the guests in the hotel were dancing.

"These trees are very old," Eva Hitchings said. She was as shadowy as the trees, as she walked beside him. "Some of them are well over a hundred years. Palms stop growing after a certain time. They say King Kamehameha landed near this grove. I remember it before the hotel was built. I liked it better then."

"It's all strange enough to me," Wilson Hitchings said. "Everything here is a little bit beyond me, if you want to know the truth. I don't know what is natural or what is artificial. I don't know what is spontaneous or what is forced. I really don't know anything."

"Don't you?" she said, and her voice was mocking. "I wonder if all deep people are as open and as frank as you are. It is becoming in a way and it's convincing. I could almost believe you, if I didn't know a great deal better."

They were by then on a cloudy, white, deserted stretch of sand, with the palm trees just behind them. She had stopped walking and was looking up at him. The wind was blowing her short, auburn hair and blowing at her dress, making her look restless and unsubstantial, although she was standing still.

"What do you know?" Wilson asked.

"Come nearer to me," Eva Hitchings said, "so I won't have to shout. That's better. Now no one else will hear." She was leaning toward him, almost touching him and her words came to him very clearly, so that there could be no doubt what he was hearing.

"I know you had a man outside in the shrubbery," she said, "who tried to shoot that poor Japanese man, Mr. Moto. I know why you want to get rid of

Mr. Moto; but I don't think it's very nice, do you? At least not for a well-bred member of the Hitchings family. I am still a little surprised, but not very much, to know that Hitchings Brothers go in for murder. But I suppose financial competition is very keen these days. Don't start, Mr. Hitchings. No one can prove anything, of course, and I won't tell anybody, yet."

If Wilson Hitchings started, he steadied himself immediately, and he was surprised at his own control; but it was probably astonishment more than will power which kept him standing, looking at her as casually as though they were speaking of the sky and sea.

"Please don't think I am shocked," Eva Hitchings was saying. "I'm quite used to the gang you have working for you at the Plantation. You did everything very nicely, except for the man you hired for murder. I can't see why you didn't do that better."

Wilson Hitchings cleared his throat.

"Now that you've been so frank," he suggested, "you'd better tell me what else you know."

"Very well," said Eva Hitchings. "You see, I'm not afraid of you, Mr. Hitchings, not one bit afraid. I know exactly why you're so anxious to buy me out, and why you want to get rid of me. Your talk about the family name is silly and we might as well both admit it. You want to buy me out so that I won't be around to find out what you are doing. Well, I won't be put out as easily as that, not until I'm ready, and I think you may as well understand it."

Wilson Hitchings felt that his heart was beating faster than it should and that his mind was moving vaguely in a cloud of stupefaction.

"Exactly what do you think I'm doing?" he asked.

"I don't mean entirely you," said Eva Hitchings. "I mean your whole family, its banking house, and all its rotten connections. Do I really have to tell you anything more?"

"I think perhaps you'd better," Wilson Hitchings said, "now that you've gone as far as this."

"All right," said Eva Hitchings. "I don't mind. It isn't any news to you, is it, that Hitchings Brothers is arranging to smuggle money into Manchuria for Chinese clients? Don't worry, I haven't told another living soul — not yet. I'm waiting until I find out a little more, and when I do, I wonder what is going to happen to the general reputation of Hitchings Brothers. It's a little late to stop me now, unless you want to kill me too. It's a little late to be sanctimonious. You're nothing but crooks, Mr. Hitchings, like a good many other business people. Do you think I have said enough?"

"Yes," said Wilson Hitchings, "almost enough. I just want to understand you clearly. What makes you think that Hitchings Brothers is doing any such thing as that?"

There must have been anger in his voice, because he felt himself growing angry, and his astonishment was leaving him, now that the first shock of incredulity was gone. He was angry, not on account of himself but on account of the aspersions which had been cast upon the family, and he knew that he was the only member of the family there to face them.

"Don't be silly," Eva Hitchings said. "Don't be honestly indignant. I know too much of the game that Hitchings Brothers is playing, and Mr. Moto knows it too. It isn't a very high-minded piece of finance; but then finance is never high-minded, if Hitchings Brothers and your father and your uncle and you are good examples."

Wilson Hitchings did not answer for a moment and he knew what she was thinking. She was thinking that his silence was a tacit acknowledgment of everything she had said; and yet in his blank surprise, he did not know what to answer. He had never realized until then that the family firm and the family were so much a part of himself that every one of her words played on his emotions. Nevertheless, he had the sense to know that an indignant denial would do no good and that she would not believe it.

She was looking at him, expecting exactly such a denial. He knew it was time for him to do something but he did not know what to do. He was trying to recall everything she had said, and to make it logical; but he could not find any definite line of logic, except that the girl was carried away by some hysterical sense of antipathy.

"Well," Eva Hitchings was saying, "I've told you where I stand. What are you going to do about it?"

Wilson Hitchings did not answer, but it was clear that he had to do something. For once in his life, circumstances were compelling him to take a definite course of action, and he found himself completely at sea, influenced more by anger than by logic. In spite of his irritation he could admire the courage of Eva Hitchings and he was ashamed to feel that he was inadequate to meet that courage. Then he remembered a piece of advice which his father had given him once — advice as conservative as the Hitchings business policy. He even remembered his father as he had given it, seated behind his desk five thousand miles away, with the tips of his fingers placed gently together.

"Sit quietly," his father had said. "Never do anything unless you know exactly what it is you are going to do."

He had always admired his father's composure

and imperturbability, without realizing that they might both be family traits. It might have been that old advice or instinct actuating him. He was never exactly sure. He stood there trying to piece unrelated facts together, trying to recall what his uncle had said of Mr. Moto in Shanghai.

"So Mr. Moto knows about this?" he asked. "Are you absolutely sure?"

"You know he does, as well as I do," Eva Hitchings answered. "Well, we've had our talk and I think I'll be going now."

He knew it was time for him to do something, even if he did not know what. She was just turning away, when he reached forward and grasped her wrist. He must have been rougher than he intended because he heard her give a cry, half of surprise and half of pain. Nevertheless, that action and the feel of Eva Hitchings' wrist inside his hand, held tightly enough so that she could not get away, made all these motives clear to him.

"Oh, no, you're not going yet," he said.

"What do you mean?" she asked, sharply. "Let go of my wrist, let it go, or else — !" She made a swift, lithe motion. She moved so suddenly that he nearly lost his grip. He had not realized that she would be so strong but he did not let her go.

"Oh, no, you don't," he said. "We're going to get

to the bottom of this before I let you go. You've made a number of accusations. I'm not thinking of myself. I am thinking of the family."

"Oh, are you?" said Eva Hitchings. "Well, you'd do a whole lot better to think about yourself. You don't know how ridiculous you sound."

"It may sound ridiculous to you," said Wilson, "but it doesn't to me. I've listened to your insinuations and every one of them is untrue and you're going to admit it before you go back to your crooked gambling house."

"Crooked?" said Eva Hitchings. "What do you mean by that?"

"Exactly what I say," Wilson answered. "If all the Hitchingses are crooked, you've inherited the trait. That wheel of yours is wired. Any sensible amateur could see it. You were fleecing one of your Chinese customers just when we were leaving. It was so crude that it was almost amusing. And we'll find out some more amusing things before we're through."

"So the pot is calling the kettle black," said Eva Hitchings; and she laughed, but her laugh was not convincing.

"If you want to deal in metaphors," Wilson told her, "the pot and the kettle are going to get shined clean. I'm going to find out exactly what you mean —and it won't do any good to wriggle."

"Then why don't you search in your own conscience?" Eva Hitchings asked — "Provided you've got a conscience. But then, all the Hitchingses are always conscientious, aren't they?"

"Yes," Wilson answered. "We're always conscientious, and I am going to do this conscientiously."

"Do what?" asked Eva Hitchings.

"I am going to call on Mr. Moto," Wilson Hitchings told her. "I am going to take you, right now, to-night, and I am going to tell him everything that you have told me, and then we'll see exactly where we stand. That's fair, isn't it?"

Eva Hitchings looked at him incredulously. "You wouldn't dare do that," she said. "You couldn't."

"You're going to find out," said Wilson, "that it's exactly what I intend to do. We're going back to your car and we're going to look for Mr. Moto. I imagine you know where he lives, as long as he came to call on you to-night."

"Suppose I don't go?" Eva Hitchings said. "Why should I?"

"If you don't," Wilson told her, "I'll know that you're afraid to back up anything that you have said. And I can probably find Mr. Moto by myself."

"You've got a good deal of impudence," Eva Hitchings said. "As a matter of fact, I wouldn't miss this for anything. You can let me go. I won't try and get away. As a matter of fact, I know exactly where Mr. Moto lives. He's staying in one of the cottages by the Seaside Hotel. It isn't far from here. We could walk, if you like."

"Very well," said Wilson. "But I hope you don't mind if I take your arm. You're a palpable fact, Miss Hitchings, and I have always been told to stick close to palpable facts."

"Very well," said Eva Hitchings, "but you're too subtle to be palpable. I suppose that makes you interesting."

"Thanks," said Wilson Hitchings. "You're rather interesting yourself. I don't know when I have had such a pleasant evening."

"Before you say that," said Eva Hitchings, "I'd wait until the evening is over."

CHAPTER VI

THEY walked up from the beach and turned to the right on a broad avenue, the name of which Wilson Hitchings had learned from his guide, that afternoon — Kalakaua Boulevard. His wrist watch showed him that the hour was 12: 15, but the street was still wide awake. In the warm darkness, it reminded Wilson almost of a street in a suburban town at home. The dark had blotted out the background and left only the doubtful imprint of America. He saw that institution, the filling station, with its pumps all lighted, exactly as they were at home, and an all night lunchroom and a drugstore. America had come to those islands, leaving as definite an impression of ideas of living as England invariably left on the outposts of the British Empire. It amused Wilson to think that the lighter ideals of his own country were stronger and more in tune with the present than those of the older nation. He recalled the jazz orchestras in the Orient, each a conscientious imitation of Broadway; and the Wild West motion pictures in Tokyo, and the baseball in Japan, and the amusement parks of Shanghai. The genius of his own nation was in them all — tawdry, superficial, but somehow strong and appealing. That genius of his country made him feel at home that night and Wilson was grateful for it, because it was something he could understand.

For the rest, he was surrounded by imponderables. The only thing he knew quite definitely was that Eva Hitchings was walking beside him. They had been thrown together involuntarily by forces which he could not understand. They were walking down the street as though they were deeply interested in each other. In a sense, perhaps, they were. She was walking quickly, without speaking, and he tried to put her from his mind as much as possible. He tried to forget the warmth and the languor of the evening. She had spoken of Manchuria and he was recalling, as clearly as he could, what his uncle had said in Shanghai. That seemed a long while ago, on the first afternoon he had met Mr. Moto.

"You may not know it," he remembered his uncle had said, "but that was a highly important call. Mr. Moto and I knew it. You heard him mention Chang Lo-Shih — that means that old Chang is meddling in Manchukuo."

He knew that Manchukuo was the new state at Manchuria but aside from that he knew nothing very definite. There was only one other thing he was sure of. No matter who else might be meddling in Manchuria, no matter what anyone else might be doing there, he knew that his own family were well out of it. His uncle had told him as much. He knew that Hitchings Brothers was not an adventurous firm. It might have been a hundred years ago, but not at present.

"What are you thinking about?" Eva Hitchings asked him.

"About what's brought us here," he said.

"Then you'd better think hard and fast," Eva Hitchings answered.

He did not reply. Although he knew that her advice was good, he was not particularly well able to follow it. He was thinking of the destiny which drew lives together. He and Eva Hitchings and Mr. Moto and the Chinese gentleman named Chang Lo-Shih whom he had seen only for a fleeting moment back in Shanghai, and the croupier and Mr. Maddock — all were drawn together in some curious, temporary relationship.

By now they had turned into a dimly lighted side street and now they were walking up a driveway.

"This is the Seaside Hotel," said Eva Hitchings, and she stopped walking. "There is the main building and there are the cottages connected with it. This isn't one of our best hotels. The place is managed by Japanese. Mr. Moto told me in his note that he is staying in Cottage 2A. Have you thought it might be dangerous to call on Mr. Moto?"

"No," said Wilson, "I hadn't. Why?"

"Well, you know best," Eva Hitchings said. "I should be if I were you."

"We're going just the same," said Wilson. "Where is the cottage?"

The main building and some of the cottages were still lit up. There were electric lights on the driveway and along the garden paths where the cottages stood, enough to show Wilson that he was in a world strange enough to him. The street outside had been primarily American but the Seaside Hotel bore the traces of Japan. There were sliding windows entirely Japanese and a pool and a Japanese garden. A girl was singing somewhere in a high falsetto voice.

"They have *sukiyaki* dinners," Eva Hitchings said. "Mostly for tourists who are interested in Japan, but a great many of the Japanese in town stay here too. We go down this walk here. . . . There's Cottage Number 2A, with the royal palm in front of it. Now what are you going to do?"

"I am going to knock on the door," Wilson Hitchings said. "I told you we were going to speak to Mr. Moto."

There was a small detached cottage in front of them. Two steps led up to a covered porch where an electric light was burning, but the windows in the cottage itself were blank and dark.

"Come on," said Wilson Hitchings. "What's the matter, are you afraid?"

"No," said Eva Hitchings. "I'm not. Are you?"

Wilson did not stop to analyze his emotions. He walked up the steps noisily and pounded on the cottage door.

"Mr. Moto," he called. "Are you in there, Mr. Moto?"

He listened, but there was no sound inside and for just a moment the silence startled him. Then he heard a voice behind him.

"Excuse me, please," the voice was saying, and Wilson Hitchings turned to the path by the cottage. Mr. Moto was standing on that path, just behind them. The light from the porch was full on his face. He was still in his evening clothes and he was bowing and smiling.

"Excuse me, please," said Mr. Moto again. "I was waiting for someone else. This is very, very nice but I am very, very much surprised." Mr. Moto moved forward quickly. "How nice of you both to come," he added. He brushed by Wilson, drawing in his breath, politely, and opened the door of his cottage, switched on a light, and bowed again. "Please, do come in," he said. "This is so very, very nice. Will you allow me to go in first?"

They followed Mr. Moto into a little sitting room, furnished with a table, a couch, and two chairs — a bare, plain enough room.

"This is so simple," said Mr. Moto. "I am so very, very sorry, but there is whisky in the bedroom."

"Never mind the whisky," Wilson Hitchings said. "What were you waiting outside for, Mr. Moto?" Mr. Moto's eyes were dark and expressionless. The gold fillings in his teeth glittered as he smiled mechanically.

"Please," he said. "I wish to see you come in to my poor house, before I came in too. Sometimes it is so very, very necessary."

"Do you do that sort of thing often?" Wilson asked.

"No," said Mr. Moto. "But sometimes it is a very useful thing to do. Several times it has saved my life. Please to sit down, Miss Hitchings. The room is poor but the weather is so pleasant. Such a lovely night. Yes, such a lovely night." Mr. Moto drew his breath through his teeth.

Eva Hitchings sat down on the couch and Wilson sat down beside her. The whole scene was becoming almost ridiculous. Now that Mr. Moto was chatting about the weather, there seemed to be no logic in it. Wilson looked at Mr. Moto and Mr. Moto looked back, bland and imperturbable.

"Well," said Wilson, "I am glad to see you, Mr.

Moto." Mr. Moto drew in his breath again, sibilantly, politely.

"And I am glad to see you," Mr. Moto said, "so very, very glad." Wilson leaned forward, trying to set his thoughts in order, but his thoughts seemed to break against the enigma of Mr. Moto, like waves against a rock.

"I suppose this is a little unusual," said Wilson. "I haven't seen much of you before. As a matter of fact, I don't exactly know who you are and I don't know what you are doing, but Miss Hitchings said a rather curious thing to-night. She intimated that it was I who had tried to kill you, Mr. Moto."

Mr. Moto moved his slender hands in a quick, disparaging gesture.

"Please," he said, "it makes so very, very little difference. So many people have tried to kill me. Please, we must all die sometime." Wilson moved impatiently, and his voice was harsher.

"But I didn't try to kill you," he said, "and I would like to know why you think I should? Why should I, Mr. Moto?"

"Please," said Mr. Moto, "there is nothing personal, of course."

"Well, there is to me," said Wilson. "Frankly, I don't like it. Back in Shanghai, my uncle told me you were a Japanese agent; is that true?"

Mr. Moto regarded him unblinkingly, with the

same, fixed nervous smile, and Eva Hitchings shrugged her shoulders, impatiently.

"Don't be so naïve," she said. "You're only making yourself ridiculous."

Wilson kept his glance on Mr. Moto. He tried to master his sense of exasperation. Of the three, he was the only one who knew nothing of what was happening and he was determined not to leave that room until he had found out something. But he had not realized the difficulty of enlisting information from a man like Mr. Moto. He could not gather from any past experience what sort of person Mr. Moto was. He could not tell whether Mr. Moto was ill at ease or not, or whether Mr. Moto's jerky, birdlike manner was natural or assumed.

"I suppose I am making myself ridiculous," Wilson Hitchings admitted, "because I know nothing, absolutely nothing. I don't understand what you are talking about, Mr. Moto, or you either, Miss Hitchings."

Eva Hitchings smiled at him through narrowing eyes. Mr. Moto rose and rubbed his hands softly together.

"It is so nice of you to say that, Mr. Hitchings," he said, "so very, very nice. It means we will have a pleasant talk. I shall be so very glad to talk; but first please, I must be hospitable. I have some whisky in my bedroom. We shall talk over a glass of whisky.

Please, do not say no. It will be so much more friendly, I think. Besides, all Americans talk business over whisky." Mr. Moto's voice broke into a sharp, artificial laugh. "Please, it would be no trouble. Please, I must insist."

Mr. Moto opened a door which apparently led to an adjoining bedroom and he was back in another moment, carrying a tray on which was a whisky bottle, a soda bottle, and two glasses. Mr. Moto's personality seemed to have changed now that he was holding a tray. He set it down on the little table with an adroit flourish that made him seem like a Japanese valet and he was quick enough to read Wilson's thoughts.

"I've served whisky so often for gentlemen in America," Mr. Moto said. "I am so very, very sorry there is no ice. Please, Miss Hitchings, you'll excuse Mr. Hitchings and me. Will you have some soda? I know so very few American ladies drink whisky."

"No," said Eva Hitchings. "Nothing for me, thanks."

"But you will excuse us, please," Mr. Moto begged. "And I am so very, very sorry there is no ice, but there is whisky, ha-ha, there is whisky, and that is the main thing, is it not? Will you say how much, Mr. Hitchings, and how much soda? Up to there? Just so? And now excuse me, I shall pour a little for myself." Mr. Moto's hands moved swiftly and accurately from bottle to glass and then he handed a glass to Wilson, bowing. It was a beautiful bow, better than a Frenchman's, Wilson thought. Mr. Moto lowered his head, slowly. His whole body seemed to droop in a gesture of complete, assumed submission and then his head and shoulders snapped up straight.

"Please," said Mr. Moto. "Thank you very very much." Wilson took the glass and nodded back. Mr. Moto was holding a glass also. He raised it and bowed again.

"To your very good health," Mr. Moto said, and Wilson was aware of a note of music in his voice, as though he were intoning a religious response. "Please, I really mean it, Mr. Hitchings." Mr. Moto's studied courtesy was amusing. In spite of himself, Wilson Hitchings smiled and did his best to respond. "Here's looking at you, Mr. Moto," he said, and he raised his glass to his lips.

The rim of the glass was just touching his lips, when something occurred so unexpectedly that he could never reconstruct it. He remembered the feel of the glass on his lips and the next instant, the glass was at his feet. The glass was lying broken, its contents were running over a woven palm-leaf mat. Mr. Moto had leapt forward and struck the glass out of Wilson's hand.

"Please," Mr. Moto was saying. "Please, excuse. I am so very, very sorry."

"Here — " Wilson began stupidly. "What's the matter, Mr. Moto?"

Mr. Moto's indrawn breath hissed obsequiously between his gold-filled teeth.

"Please," said Mr. Moto, "I hope you will forgive me. Everything is so very, very clear now. I could not believe that you would mean to drink. Please, I believe you now. I believe that you know nothing, Mr. Hitchings. You are very, very honest. Yes, excuse me, please."

Wilson Hitchings was still seated on the couch.

"Of course, I meant to drink it," he said. "Why shouldn't I?"

"Please," said Mr. Moto again. "Excuse me, I have been so very, very stupid. Please, let me explain. That whisky, I left it on my bureau. I nearly always take a little before my bedtime. Excuse me; this evening, I came home to find that the whisky was poisoned with cyanide of potassium. Please, you may smell a little, if you like. The odor is so very distinctive; one has to be so careful, always. Now, I know that you know nothing, Mr. Hitchings — and I must apologize to you very, very much. Now, I can believe anything you say."

Wilson Hitchings felt that his forehead was growing moist.

"You mean," he said — "you mean, you thought that I had done *that?*"

"Please," said Mr. Moto. "Not you, but I thought, perhaps, you knew who did. Please, Mr. Hitchings, I am so very, very sorry."

Then Eva Hitchings was speaking to him and he saw that her face was pale.

"You were going to drink it," she said, almost mechanically. "You were really going to drink it. I didn't know about it, I swear I didn't know." She reached out her hand and placed it gently on his knee. "I'm awfully sorry for anything I have said," she added. "I guess I have been an awful fool. Will you forgive me? I'd have believed anything out of a Hitchings."

Wilson Hitchings smiled but he felt very cold inside. The significance of everything was dawning on him, slowly.

"So you take back what you said?" he asked her.

"Yes," she answered steadily, "I take back everything."

Wilson Hitchings sat up straighter.

"Well," he said stiffly, "I'm glad you do. And now I'll tell you something, and you too, Mr. Moto. The Hitchingses mean what they say. We're pretty honest on the whole. I should have been glad to have swallowed that whole glass, if it could have helped the family."

Mr. Moto rubbed his hands. "That is very nice," he said. "It is so very Japanese. It is very, very nice."

Eva Hitchings drew her hand away.

"Can't you ever get away from your family, even for a minute?" she asked. "Don't be such a prig! Who cares about your family?"

Mr. Moto was on his knee picking up the bits of broken glass.

"I do," said Wilson. "I care."

"Well, I don't," said Eva Hitchings. "I don't care a button. I only know you nearly killed yourself."

"Oh, no," said Mr. Moto. "Please. I was watching carefully. I was watching all the time. Poison is so common sometimes, that one must be very, very careful. Now I think we had better talk quite quickly, if you please, because I think whoever fixed that whisky will be coming here and I want to know who it is so very, very much. That was why I was waiting outside when you came in to call."

"Are you going to tell me what this is all about, or aren't you?" Wilson asked. "You'll excuse me, Mr. Moto, but I'm getting very much confused."

Mr. Moto was pouring some soda water over his fingers and was rubbing them dry with his handkerchief. "Yes," said Mr. Moto, "I should be so pleased to tell you everything, now that everything is so very nice. You're quite right, Mr. Hitchings, I have come here to do a little work for my country. I shall be so very pleased to tell you but I must think a moment. Someone will be coming here, coming very soon, I think. There must not be too much noise. I must speak very softly, so that I can listen. Let me listen, please."

Wilson Hitchings could hear nothing but the sound of the wind outside and if Mr. Moto heard more than that, it could have been nothing to disturb him.

"I think," said Mr. Moto, softly, "it would be well to keep our voices down, for things are a little bit mixed up. Just answer me softly if you do not mind. Please tell me why you came to Honolulu when I did, Mr. Hitchings? That is what made me think wrong things. Did you know that I was coming?"

Wilson Hitchings shook his head.

"I hadn't the least idea," he answered; "and I don't mind telling you my reason. I was sent here because Miss Hitchings was running Hitchings Plantation. Its name, being the same name as Hitchings Brothers, was interfering with the reputation of the firm. I was sent to try to buy Miss Hitchings out, and to have the establishment closed."

Mr. Moto raised his eyebrows slightly and his forehead wrinkled.

"You actually wish the place closed?" he repeated. "You had no other reason to come here?"

"Absolutely none," said Wilson. "Don't you believe me, Mr. Moto?"

Mr. Moto rubbed his hands together and the wrinkles in his forehead deepened.

"Then there must be someone else," he said. "Yes, there must be someone else. I thought it might be Miss Hitchings, but since she is here with you, I do not think so. It did not seem right from the first. I should have known Hitchings Brothers was too old a house, that it could not afford to take such a risk, that it would not. I am very, very sorry."

Wilson Hitchings leaned forward, impatiently.

"It seems to me," he said, "that you are either very glad or sorry about something, all the time. Is it possible for you to be direct? I don't know who you are, Mr. Moto, and I don't much care, but I would like to know what you are sorry about."

The wrinkles left Mr. Moto's forehead and his cheeks creased in another smile.

"I am beginning to be very, very sorry for you, Mr. Hitchings. They would be anxious to liquidate me, of course, under the circumstances; and now, if you wish to buy the place, they may wish to kill you also. It is very, very funny how things sometimes grow confused."

It seemed to Wilson Hitchings that the room had grown hot and close. He took a handkerchief from his pocket and mopped his forehead. He was surprised that Mr. Moto's remark had no great effect on him, rather it confirmed something which he had been suspecting.

"Who are they?" he asked.

Mr. Moto looked at him rather sharply and shrugged his shoulders.

"Certain persons who are not very nice, I'm afraid," he said. "Excuse me; when I saw you first, I could not believe that you knew so little. You are, without knowing it, in a situation which is not very nice. I do not mind telling you frankly, and perhaps you will understand. I speak for my country, Mr. Hitchings, and I am here for it. You know of the new nation of Manchukuo, in which my own country has been so much interested?"

"Yes," said Wilson, "everyone knows that; but it seems to me you are getting a little far away."

"That is just it." Mr. Moto rubbed his hands again. "This is so far away that one might not connect the two. Manchukuo is a nice country. It is very, very beautiful and I have had many pleasant times there. It is too bad that there is so much trouble in it. There are still a good many bandits in the mountains. Certain persons have been causing factions to make trouble lately. Certain Chinese and certain persons of another power. Am I being too vague, Mr. Hitchings?"

"Yes," said Wilson. "You certainly are, Mr. Moto."

"Please," said Mr. Moto. "I shall try to be more

clear. It has been known for some time that large amounts of money are being passed from China to certain insurgent leaders in the mountains. It has been my duty for some months now to try to trace the paths through which that money goes. It has been my duty to try to block those paths. It has been very, very hard. Do you understand me better, Mr. Hitchings?"

"No, I don't," Wilson Hitchings told him.

"Please," said Mr. Moto, "I hope that you will in just a moment. The channel through which the money first passed was stopped six months ago, I do not think it will be reopened again." Mr. Moto paused and smiled. "At least not by the same person. Fortunately such matters can be arranged very easily over there. Here it is so much more difficult. When that channel was stopped, I and my associates were much surprised to find that sums of money were still coming in. This time American dollars were appearing. We did not know from where. Then I began looking into the affairs of a Chinese gentleman, named Chang Lo-Shih. Do you remember that I mentioned him, Mr. Hitchings, in Shanghai?"

"Yes," said Wilson. "I remember."

"He is not a very nice gentleman," Mr. Moto said. "He does not appreciate my country or understand its aims. He has been handling a great deal of that money." Mr. Moto paused and sighed. "Just a little while ago, I found that this Mr. Chang has been sending large sums of money to an account in the Hitchings office here."

"If you'll excuse me," said Wilson. "I don't quite see the connection."

Mr. Moto bobbed his shining black head in a polite gesture of assent.

"Please," he said, "that is what I am looking for. That is what I am hoping to find: the exact connection. Perhaps you do not understand. These matters are so misleading, so intricate, so very, very difficult. In your own great country, Mr. Hitchings, perhaps you have read of the investigations into the bank accounts of gangsters and unworthy politicians. It is so very, very interesting the way a clever man can cover the trail of money. Sometimes it seems to be thrown like water upon the desert sand. It evaporates and yet somewhere it condenses back again into money. As I say, I am looking for the connection. I and my associates have been looking for it very, very hard. Now here is one thing we have noticed. We have noticed American dollars in many sections of the nation of Manchukuo. They drift into the banks for exchange, a little here and there. This has struck us as being a little odd. There is no reason, of course, why a Chinese in Shanghai should not have banking connections here. Mr. Chang is a businessman and there are many Chinese businessmen in

Honolulu. It is such an interesting city. Now, let me tell you something else."

"I wish you would," said Wilson.

"We have found," said Mr. Moto, slowly and softly, "that this money which Mr. Chang is sending here is being employed for a purpose which is a little unusual. It represents the capital of a gambling syndicate. A representative of this gambling syndicate has been drawing upon it for gambling purposes at Hitchings Plantation. I hope I am being clearer now, Mr. Hitchings. We know through our sources of information that American money comes to Manchuria through Japan from vessels which have touched at this port. I do not need to go into the details or the methods. They would not be very interesting. But what is very interesting to me is that Mr. Chang has been sending money here. It goes to Hitchings Plantation. Where does it go from there? That is what I should like so very much to know?"

"If that's all you know," Wilson Hitchings said, "it seems to me you're only guessing, Mr. Moto. It seems to me you're only shooting in the dark."

Mr. Moto bobbed his head and smiled.

"Ha-ha," he said, "that is a very nice joke, shooting in the dark. So much has to be done by guessing, Mr. Hitchings, the way things are to-day. I guess and guess and then sometimes I guess right, and can you think how I know?"

"How?" asked Wilson. "By your native intuition?"

"Please," said Mr. Moto. "There is something more than that. I am sure that I am right; very, very sure, when someone starts shooting at me in the dark. Please, do you remember? Someone did to-night when I called at Miss Hitchings' lovely place. Did someone, Miss Hitchings?"

Eva Hitchings did not answer but she nodded. Mr. Moto's expressionless eyes were on her and Wilson watched their glances meet and saw her look away.

"Don't you think that is a rather dangerous way of finding out things?" Wilson Hitchings inquired.

"Please," said Mr. Moto. "So many things I do are dangerous. Besides, if I found out what I wish, I should be very, very pleased to die. If I do not find out, I am afraid that I must kill myself, so that all is very much the same."

"You don't look like a fanatic," Wilson Hitchings said.

"I am not," said Mr. Moto. "The day before you arrived, Mr. Hitchings, for I traveled very fast to get here, I called on the lady who is with you. She asked me to come back to-night. She said that she would tell me something that would interest me. She said that she did not like your family, Mr. Hitchings."

"That's true, I don't," Eva Hitchings said.

"You were present at the interview to-night," Mr. Moto continued, "and now I think you can understand my line of thought. You arrived quite suddenly, Mr. Hitchings. Mr. Chang had an account at Hitchings Brothers here. His money was used at that very nice gambling table and I was shot at in the dark. Please excuse me for suspecting you, Mr. Hitchings. Perhaps you will agree that it was natural. Hitchings Brothers and Hitchings Plantation seemed quite the same to me and very, very clever. Now I know that I was wrong. Nevertheless, the only thing I need to know now, I am very, very sure, is how Mr. Chang's money disappears at Hitchings Plantation and appears in Manchukuo.

"It has been a very clever and a very unusual device, that way of passing money, and a difficult method to trace. That is its great advantage. Please, may I make myself clearer? Usually in such cases, a sum of money is passed from one person to another. The person who receives it may be identified eventually by suitable police methods, but here it is like water thrown on sand. These funds disappear across the table to a number of different persons or to the house. I do not quite know how the method is worked. It is not perhaps important, but there is one thing of which I am now very sure. The money which is lost from Mr. Chang's account is collected all together and is given to a single individual who comes here at intervals and takes it away. I believe he is coming quite soon. When I find who that person is, the whole plan will break down. A few simple words over the cable to suitable authorities will make it possible to have him stopped. The person who finally takes the money — his identity is all that I wish to know."

Mr. Moto paused and rubbed his hands.

"Please," he said, "Miss Hitchings, will you tell me now what you were going to say to-night?"

Eva Hitchings clasped her hands together in her lap and sat up straight, then she shook her head.

"I think you know enough already, Mr. Moto," she answered. Her voice was cool and hard. "And I think you're so clever that I don't need to tell you anything. I was almost taken in by your trick about the whisky. I think you'll be able to manage Mr. Hitchings very well by yourself and perhaps I had better leave you, so that you won't be embarrassed. I think I'll be going now."

For a moment Wilson Hitchings found it difficult to speak.

"Don't you believe me?" he said. "Don't you believe me at all?"

Eva Hitchings' glance was cold and self-possessed. She pushed a strand of hair from her forehead, folded her hands again.

"If you really want to know what I think," she said, "I think you're the smoothest liar since Ananias. I think you can tell Mr. Moto exactly what's happening to that money, and I rather think that Mr. Moto knows that you can tell him. I still believe what I told you on the beach, Mr. Hitchings. You never meant to touch that drink on the table — did you?"

For the first time that day Wilson Hitchings realized that he was very tired. He felt a weariness which numbed his ability to reason and it placed him beyond surprise and beyond incredulity.

"I don't exactly understand you," he said.

Eva Hitchings shrugged her bare, brown shoulders.

"I've noticed that you don't understand anything," she remarked. "You're quite attractive when you are naïve. I imagine Mr. Moto understands you. I don't think you've fooled either of us."

"Yes," said Mr. Moto. "Thank you very much." He seemed about to continue, and then he stopped and lowered his voice to a whisper.

"Be quiet, please," he whispered. "Do not say a word, please. Sit just as you are. Someone is coming up the path."

Then Wilson knew that Mr. Moto must have been listening all the time and that his ears were very keen. For several seconds Wilson could hear nothing except that soft, ceaseless, tropical trade wind which seemed to form a background to all life, and then he heard a footstep; a quick, decisive footstep. The sound made him move uneasily.

"Quiet," hissed Mr. Moto. "Quiet, please!" There was an insistence in Mr. Moto's whisper which made him absolutely still and Eva Hitchings' face made him even quieter. Her face was a little pale. Her lips were half-parted and her self-confidence and irony were gone with the sound of the footsteps. They were coming nearer. They stopped and Wilson knew that someone was pausing before the window of the cottage. Then there was another sound. Whoever it was outside was walking up the porch steps directly to the door.

The back of Wilson's neck was cold and his mouth was dry, and if he had tried, he could not have moved just then. Mr. Moto was standing on the palm mat in the center of the room, still with a faint mechanical smile. Softly but deliberately, Mr. Moto thrust his right hand into the side pocket of his coat. The steps had stopped by the door and again there was not a sound except for the wind. Then there was a rapping on the door. The sound seemed very loud in the stillness of the room but Mr. Moto did not move or speak. Then the knob of the door turned and the door was opened briskly.

Wilson could not have said what he expected to see, but the actual sight was a complete anticlimax. A man stood in the doorway, dressed in a light linen suit and wearing a panama hat that had a band of feathers around it, a peculiar product of the islands which Wilson had already noticed. A thin, oldish man, with a close-cropped mustache and a lean, tan face. . . . Wilson remembered the droop of the mouth, half good-natured, half querulous, and the benign, rather lazy cast of the eyes. It was Mr. Wilkie, the Office Manager of Hitchings Brothers, standing in the door. Mr. Wilkie stood for a moment, quite motionless, as though the light confused him.

"Excuse me," he said quickly. "I was looking for —" and then he saw Eva Hitchings. It was plain that he had not noticed her at first, because his voice changed.

"Why, Eva," said Mr. Wilkie — "so there you are, you little hide-and-seek. I've been looking for you everywhere!"

Eva Hitchings stood up and she laughed a quick, nervous laugh of complete relief.

"Why, Uncle Joe," she said, "you didn't need to look. I don't need a caretaker!" She rose and walked toward him, still laughing, and Mr. Wilkie placed his arm around her shoulders.

"Oh, yes, you do," he said. "At least I think you do. Good evening, Mr. Hitchings. Eva always seems like a little girl to me, like my own little girl. I still get worried when she's out alone at night. They told me that she'd taken you home, Mr. Hitchings, and when she did not come back, well, I thought that I might as well go and find her. Of course nothing can hap-

pen to anyone on these Islands, not since King Kamehameha lay down the law that women and children
were safe wherever they went; but there is a time for
girls to go to bed, even nowadays. I saw Eva's car
by the hotel and walked over to the beach, then one
of the boys over at the filling station told me that
they had seen Eva coming here, and one of the boys
at the Seaside had seen her walk this way. And I
knew that Eva was at her old tricks again, forgetting
what time it was, forgetting that it was after one
o'clock; so the old man has come to take her home.
I am sure that Mr. Hitchings understands."

"Certainly," said Wilson. "I was just about to take
her back myself, Mr. Wilkie. We just stopped in to
call on Mr. Moto. My uncle introduced me to him in
Shanghai."

"Yes," said Mr. Moto. "It has been so very nice and
it is so nice of you to come, sir. May I not offer you a
glass of whisky, Mr. — Mr. . . . ?"

"Mr. Wilkie," said Wilson. "Excuse me; this is
Mr. Wilkie, Mr. Moto, the Manager of Hitchings
Brothers' Branch."

Mr. Moto bowed.

"I am so honored," he said, "so very, very honored. I have been to call on Mr. Wilkie, but twice he
was out. Please, will you not have some whisky, Mr.
Wilkie?"

"No, thank you," Mr. Wilkie said. "Some other

time, but not to-night. I've just come to take my little girl away. If you are ready, Eva?"

"All right, Uncle Joe," said Eva. "Good night, Mr. Moto. Good night, Mr. Hitchings."

Mr. Moto stood at his doorway, watching the two walk down the path — for a longer time, it seemed to Wilson, than was necessary. Then Mr. Moto closed the door gently and looked at Wilson Hitchings. His face was tranquil and passive, and he was not smiling. He had withdrawn his right hand from his pocket and was rubbing both his hands together gently, in a curious half-submissive gesture.

Wilson walked to the tray with the whisky bottle.

"Well," he said, "I'll have a drink now, if you don't mind?"

Mr. Moto did not move but he spoke very gently.

"First," he said, "I think you had better smell that whisky carefully, Mr. Hitchings, and then if you are tired of life, pour yourself a little in the glass. Everything will be over reasonably quickly, although the effect of cyanide is not as rapid as is usually supposed. It depends on the condition of the individual and when he has eaten. Nevertheless it is a very, very deadly poison — but you are an educated man; I do not need to tell you that."

"Then you weren't fooling me?" Wilson Hitchings asked — "The way she said?"

"No," said Mr. Moto. "That would be what you

call in your country a cheap trick. I am not cheap, Mr. Hitchings, at least not very often, I hope.

"No. Mr. Hitchings, please, I have meant what I said to you and I have believed exactly what you said. You know nothing about this matter and I am very, very glad that it is so. Will you permit me, if I give you now my humble but best advice?"

Mr. Moto walked closer to Wilson Hitchings.

"I have believed you, Mr. Hitchings," he said, "but I am very, very sorry that I do not believe the young lady. I am so sorry to say that I do not think she is very nice. I should be very careful of her, Mr. Hitchings. I should not see her again."

Wilson Hitchings was surprised at his own answer. He was indignant without knowing that he would be.

"You're wrong there," he said, earnestly. "I'll guarantee you that Miss Hitchings has nothing to do with this, absolutely nothing. There's no doubt there is a bad element in that place of hers, because I have seen some of them myself. I suppose a bad crowd gets into every such establishment; but it isn't Miss Hitchings' fault. She accused me of being mixed up in this. She would hardly do that, if she were involved."

"Why not?" said Mr. Moto gently. "Please, will you answer me why not?"

Wilson scowled and was surprised. He found Mr. Moto's question hard to answer.

"Well, she wouldn't," he said. "She's honest, Mr. Moto."

Mr. Moto blinked and for the first time it seemed to Wilson Hitchings that there was genuine amusement in Mr. Moto's smile.

"Excuse me," he said, "please, excuse me, Mr. Hitchings, if I say something which is not very, very nice. Please, I have been to very many places in both Europe and America during the course of my work and my education. I have seen many types of people and there is one thing I have observed about your great country, Mr. Hitchings. You do not treat women very realistically. You think they are all very nice, because they are women. You think Miss Hitchings is very nice. Why? Because you think she is beautiful. You like her wide violet eyes. You enjoy the flame color in her hair and no doubt the way she swings herself when she walks. Excuse me, please. I come from a race with a tradition which is very, very different. Excuse me, I do not think Miss Hitchings is beautiful at all. Please, that is why I can see her more clearly than you do, Mr. Hitchings. A beautiful woman is so very, very confusing to a man. He desires her. Excuse me for my rudeness, but you desire Miss Hitchings."

"I don't," said Wilson Hitchings, quickly. "I don't, at all. I am only trying to be fair."

"I hope so much that you will excuse me, please, when I make myself so very rude as to contradict, because I do it to be nice. She interests you, Mr. Hitchings, very, very much; and she knows it — women always know. She is playing with you, Mr. Hitchings. She is clever to put the blame on you because she thinks I may be deceived by it. Believe me, I am not deceived. She is in company which is not very nice. No one in that company can be nice."

"Now, wait a minute," Wilson interrupted. "Miss Hitchings is a distant relative of mine. She's had a hard time. Her father lost his money."

Mr. Moto shrugged his shoulders.

"Please," he said. "Please, stop, Mr. Hitchings. All such persons have an interesting history which is very, very sad. The life of everyone, I think, is very, very sad; but misfortune must not interfere with logic. It is fortunate for you, I think, that she came here with you to-night, because I can help you very much. You have come only to close the Hitchings Plantation. Honolulu is so very, very beautiful. There are so very many things to do. Amuse yourself, please, after this. Bathe in the warm seas. See the other pretty girls. Listen to the lovely music. Sit in the sun and think, but not about this affair, Mr. Hitchings. You are out of it, now. I think, when I

154

am through, that Miss Hitchings will be very, very glad to close her establishment. And now that matters have gone as far as this, they will move very, very quickly. Please, you need not give it another thought. You only have to wait."

Mr. Moto lighted a cigarette.

"Yes," he said. "This is my business. You only have to wait."

In spite of his small size, Mr. Moto looked grimly adequate and Wilson Hitchings could understand his logic. What he could not understand was his own reluctance to agree. Although he knew that Mr. Moto was right, he knew that he could not leave things as they were. He tried to think it was a sense of responsibility which prompted him, but he knew it was not that. It had something to do with the grim finality of Mr. Moto's voice. He did not want to leave Eva Hitchings to Mr. Moto. He wanted to attend to Eva Hitchings himself. He wanted to see her again. He wanted to speak to her again, and it was utterly unthinkable that he should not be allowed to do it.

"You're wrong, Mr. Moto," he said. "I'm in this as much as you."

"Please," said Mr. Moto. "I do not understand."

"I am out here to represent my family," Wilson said. "I was sent here to deal with Miss Hitchings, and I am going to."

"Please," said Mr. Moto. "It is dangerous. There is no need."

"Never mind," said Wilson Hitchings. "I am going to. You needn't worry about me, Mr. Moto."

"I shall be sorry for you," said Mr. Moto. "Very, very sorry. What are you going to do?"

"To-morrow morning," Wilson said, "I am going to speak to Mr. Wilkie."

"I should not do that," said Mr. Moto. "It will do no good."

"Well, I am going to," Wilson Hitchings said.

"Please, may I give you a present? You will need it very much, I think." Mr. Moto's hand moved to his pocket. He was holding out an automatic pistol.

"Nonsense," said Wilson. "I won't need that. No, thank you. Good night, Mr. Moto."

"You are sure you will not take it?" Mr. Moto said. "You may need it even before you get to your hotel. Good night, Mr. Hitchings. I am so very, very sorry."

It was after two in the morning when Wilson Hitchings reached his room in his hotel and locked the door very carefully behind him. Once he was inside his room, where all his personal belongings lay methodically and neatly according to his habit, nearly everything which had happened that day assumed grotesque proportions. The wind and the sound of the surf on the reef had dropped to a lazy reassuring murmur and he could feel around him nothing but security. It was the old security in which he had been bred and reared, where nothing happened which was unusual — nothing which was not the result of balanced thought and plan. Viewed in that perspective, the entire day and night seemed to move beyond his mental grasp as something to be discounted, as something which had not actually occurred; and now his mind was busy proving that many things meant nothing. The impressions which were crowded on him were too numerous to be assimilated and his mind was tossing half of those impressions into discard. The internal struggles in the former province of Manchuria were too far beyond him to disturb him any more than the threats that Mr. Moto made of personal danger. He could believe it was complete exaggeration now that he was alone. The faces and the voices which he had heard, now that he was trying to get to sleep, had become as unconvincing as those of actors in a badly directed play. There was only one face of the entire gallery which remained with him as evidence of actual experience.

He could not, although he tried deliberately, push Eva Hitchings from his mind. She was so entirely different from anything he imagined that his thoughts dwelt on her speculatively. He could still hear the irony of her voice. He could recall the way the light glittered in her hair. He could remember a dozen half-graceful, half-careless gestures: the way she had pulled petulantly at the shoulder strap of that red dress with white flowers, the contemptuous ease with which she had driven her car, the way her eyes had met his squarely, more like a man's eyes than a woman's. Hers was the only face in that gallery which stood out distinctly and which had nothing furtive about it, nothing deceitful, and nothing ugly. And he knew why she was distinct to him and he knew that his conviction was not induced by sentiment as Mr. Moto had said. It was because she did not belong with those others, because she had an integrity which all those others lacked. She had been completely frank with him on her likes and dislikes. She did not belong there. She was entirely alone. There had been moments, too, when he believed she was afraid; and in a sense he felt responsible for that isolation of hers because, in a way, it was the fault of his own family. He knew that he could not leave her and keep his conscience clear, without giving her another chance to get away from the situation in which she was placed. He was convinced that his intuition was right, that she was in some sort of trouble.

He closed his eyes and he could hear the music at Hitchings Plantation. Then the music died out and he seemed to be back in that dark-paneled room with the green rays of the gaming table beneath its hard white light. He could hear the clinking of the counters and the soft whirr of the wheel and the oily-faced croupier was saying: *"Rien ne va plus."*

He knew that the wheel was crooked. There was not much doubt that one of the men beside it could manipulate it, so that the house could either win or lose. That was the last thing he remembered thinking before he fell asleep.

CHAPTER VII

H<small>E</small> was awakened by the ringing of his telephone. His sleep must have been very light, because the sound of the jangling bell ran through him like a shock of electricity that aroused him to complete and instant consciousness. Yet, in spite of his awareness of everything around him, he had that sensation, that everyone must have experienced at sometime or other, of a temporary lack of memory, of not knowing exactly where he was. The room was full of sunlight, the breeze was blowing the curtain of his open window and he heard that restless perpetual sound of the sea. He almost believed that he was at home on a June morning until he saw his dressing-case on his bureau and heard the sea. He was still trying to gather his thoughts together when he picked up the telephone. A girl's voice was speaking in a mechanical, impersonal way — peculiar to the switchboard operator of a large office or hotel.

"Mr. Hitchings," the operator was saying, "there's

a man downstairs who wants to see you. His name is Mr. Maddock."

"Mr. — who?" said Wilson.

"Mr. Maddock," the operator said. "Shall I tell him to go up?"

Then everything came back to Wilson Hitchings. The telephone had awakened his body and now the name had awakened everything in his mind. He remembered Mr. Maddock very clearly and not very pleasantly. He looked at his watch and found it was after ten o'clock.

"Send him up," said Wilson, "and send up a waiter, please. I want some breakfast." He shoved his bare feet into his slippers and put on a silk dressing-gown and looked at himself carefully in the mirror, as he brushed his straight, brown hair. He was pleased to see that his face looked serene, although he felt very much disturbed. He sat down with his back to the open window, with an empty chair opposite him, waiting.

"You must be very careful," he said to himself. "You must try to use your mind." He tried to use his mind while he waited. He tried to recall everything he had observed about Mr. Maddock, none of which was particularly reassuring, but he did not have long to wait. Mr. Maddock rapped on the door. When Wilson told him to come in, his visitor edged himself sideways through the half-open door and closed it softly behind him. There was a smoothness and a caution about Mr. Maddock's entrance which made Wilson wonder whether the action was instinctive or assumed. Mr. Maddock's yellowish eyes focused themselves studiously upon the details of the room before he spoke.

"Hi," said Mr. Maddock and he waved a skinny arm in a genial, loose-jointed gesture. His Adam's apple moved convulsively and he smiled, a swift, confidential smile.

"Hi," said Wilson Hitchings, and examined Mr. Maddock, as Mr. Maddock continued to examine the room. Mr. Maddock looked as stringy as ever, but he was beautifully turned out in a fresh light-tan Palm Beach suit which fitted closely around his narrow waist. His shoes were white buckskin, his tie was a salmon-colored foulard, his black hair was glossed to a patent-leather finish.

"Nice rooms they have here," Mr. Maddock said.

Wilson pointed to the empty chair.

"You can sit down there, if you want to," Wilson told him, "and a waiter will be up in just a minute to take my order for breakfast. I thought perhaps you'd like to know."

Mr. Maddock sat down and adjusted the creases of his trousers and stared at Wilson, unblinkingly.

"Wise guy, ain't you?" Mr. Maddock said, "and I suppose you're going to write on the order blank to have the house dick waiting in the corridor. Yea, I spotted you for a wise guy. Skip it, pal. There's no rough stuff. This is a purely social, confidential call, and I think you'll like it, pal, really I do."

Wilson smiled brightly at Mr. Maddock.

"No poison in the whisky, Mr. Maddock?" he inquired. It was a shot in the dark and he knew it, but his question did not appear to surprise Mr. Maddock in the least. He raised his dark eyebrows slightly and his long fingers hung limply on the arms of his chair.

"You go around nights, don't you, pal?" said Mr. Maddock, softly.

"Sometimes," Wilson said.

Mr. Maddock leaned his head against the chair-back and half-closed his yellow eyes.

"Listen, pal," he said. "I'm a guy who's got to be careful. I am always careful, that's why I'm here on the damn Island with the ukeleles and the grass skirts and not back home where I belong. I got too much on my own mind for rough stuff. Besides, I don't like it on an island, wise guy. Guess why if you want to." Mr. Maddock made his fingers move in an engaging wavelike gesture. "Too much water. It's too damn hard to get off an island, and there's one island I don't want to try getting off of — Alcatraz Island, San Francisco Bay. . . . Snow, pal, if you don't get my drift."

"I suppose you mean to imply that you have a
163

criminal record, Mr. Maddock," said Wilson, and he felt more at ease than he had, because Mr. Maddock's cool indolence was reassuring. He even found himself growing interested in Mr. Maddock, and aware that he was faced with an unusual opportunity to study an unknown world. "You really didn't need to tell me, Mr. Maddock," Wilson continued. "I guessed as soon as I saw you that you were on the Public Enemy list."

"Okay, pal," said Mr. Maddock, softly. "All this is just a big vacation. This racket is small-time. . . . Snow, if you don't get my drift."

"Very well," said Wilson, "I'll snow if I don't. Please go on, Mr. Maddock."

Mr. Maddock opened his eyes dreamily and half-closed them again.

"The spot is getting hot," said Mr. Maddock gently. "I don't want no steam room. I want ear muffs. . . . Snow, if you don't get my drift."

"You are fond of that expression, aren't you, Mr. Maddock?"

Mr. Maddock closed his eyes.

"Yes," he said; "but I don't use snow, pal, and I don't drink or smoke and I don't step out with any finger molls. I am always God-damn careful."

"It's nice of you to be so frank," Wilson said. "You make me feel so much easier. Do you live at the Y.M.C.A., Mr. Maddock?"

Mr. Maddock's lips curled upward and his shoulders shook but he made no sound of merriment.

"Funny guy, pal, aren't you?" he said. "And you got a damn dead pan. It's comical, you're kind of new to me."

"You're new to me too, Mr. Maddock," Wilson Hitchings said. "But snow, if you don't get my drift."

"I've never snowed yet," Mr. Maddock said. "I've never snowed on anybody, pal. You're a wise guy. You and me can play."

"Play what?" asked Wilson Hitchings.

"Ball," said Mr. Maddock. "Ball, pal." Mr. Maddock half-closed his eyes again and sighed and Wilson Hitchings could feel his own interest growing. At any rate, he was playing a word game with Mr. Maddock and experimenting purely with an unknown quantity and beginning to delve incredulously into Mr. Maddock's past.

"Do I understand that you are making me a proposition?" he inquired.

Mr. Maddock gazed at the fingers on his right hand, blew softly on his fingernails and polished them on his coat sleeve.

"Pierre and I were talking about you last night," he said. "You'd really like Pierre."

"I'm afraid I don't know him," Wilson said.

"The guy who speaks French," Mr. Maddock explained. "The croupier at the table last night. He's a pal of mine. You'd really like Pierre."

There was a knock on the door. It was the waiter with the menu card.

"Will you join me?" Wilson asked.

"Sure," said Mr. Maddock. "A glass of hot milk, please." Mr. Maddock closed his eyes and sighed, but when the waiter was gone, he opened them again.

"First Pierre and me placed you for a college boy," said Mr. Maddock, and his voice was more incisive; "then we didn't, when you played the wheel."

"It's a crooked wheel, isn't it?" said Wilson.

Mr. Maddock sighed again. "Yes," he said, "it's crooked, pal. Don't act dumb, pal. It's so crooked that it's hot. It's too damn hot and I don't like the crowd. When they propositioned me, I fell for it as a straight gambling proposition, when it ain't. Them Russians and them Chinks — they're too damn jumpy, pal. I'm used to big shots who keep cool. They got the jitters and they tried to kill the Jap last night. You know, you're wise. Well, an island ain't no place. First that Jap guy comes. Then you come, and now the little lady is getting wise. There isn't anybody out there at the dump with a business head. They haven't been in the wars, like I've been, pal. They got the jitters and they're going to blow wide open. There's no executive ability. Pierre and me, we're going to lam. Snow, if you don't get my drift."

Wilson Hitchings watched Mr. Maddock's unblinking yellowish eyes.

"You're being rather frank, aren't you?" he inquired.

"Yes," said Mr. Maddock. "Because I'm too hot for trouble, pal. I'm just looking for the angle where I can cash and lam."

The waiter came with the breakfast tray and Mr. Maddock closed his eyes again. Then he sipped his hot milk, daintily, and drew a purple handkerchief from his breast pocket and wiped his lips.

"And you've come to me for cash?" Wilson Hitchings suggested.

Mr. Maddock set down his glass of milk.

"Yes; you or the Jap, pal," he said; "and when I cross I'd rather cross to a white man. I set you down for a right guy, pal. Here's the picture. Snow, if you don't get my drift."

"Go ahead," said Wilson. "Don't let me stop you, Mr. Maddock."

Mr. Maddock sat up straighter and his fingers closed gently around the arms of his chair.

"Last night you propositioned the little lady," Mr. Maddock said, "because the name of her house hurts your business. You propositioned her to buy for a hundred grand and close it out. The little lady turned you down."

"You think so?" said Wilson, carefully. "How do you know that?"

"Don't worry, pal," said Mr. Maddock. "The crowd's got ways of knowing. They don't want the house closed just yet, but I can tell you something that can close it, pal. The authorities" — Mr. Maddock drew out his handkerchief and wiped his lips — "won't stand for the racket unless it is quiet and refined. They've said as much. Well, here's the proposition, pal. I know something that will close that house so tight it will never open. No one would dare to open it and it won't cost you a hundred grand either to know it, pal. Five grand is my price and you can pay either by personal check or cash. You can close the little lady out for five grand and she's through. She's only the front, pal. She's not worth a hundred grand and I'm putting it to you straight. If you don't think what I tell you is worth the money, you tell me. How about it, pal? Snow, if you don't get my drift."

"You mean you're going to squeal?" Wilson Hitchings asked.

"Yes," said Mr. Maddock. "I mean I am going to squeal."

Wilson Hitchings lighted a cigarette and thought carefully what he would say next.

"I suppose," he spoke slowly, watching Mr. Maddock, "you're going to tell me that money is being sent to Manchuria. It isn't worth the price. I know it already, Mr. Maddock."

The Adam's apple moved in Mr. Maddock's throat. He opened his eyes and half-closed them.

"Wise guy," he said, "ain't you, pal?"

"Do you think so?" Wilson Hitchings asked. "It never occurred to me until I came here that I was particularly wise."

Mr. Maddock nodded dreamily.

"Yea, I think you are," he said. "I think you're a damn wise guy. Any time you want a job back home in a real organization, I might put in a word for you. You've told me all I need to know. I'm picking up the marbles, pal, and calling it a day. They got a Hawaiian word for it out here. I'm *pau*. That means I'm washing up. Kind of tough on the little lady, too. She had a nice layout before we muscled in, but I guess she's *pau*. Thanks for the information."

"You're very welcome," Wilson Hitchings said. He could guess without exactly knowing what Mr. Maddock was thanking him for. He could believe that Mr. Maddock was speaking the exact truth, and that someone knew too much. Already someone

169

knew too much about money going into Manchuria and Wilson could guess who it was. He was very sure that the work in which Mr. Maddock was engaged was genuinely distasteful to him.

Mr. Maddock half-reclined in his chair and gave no sign of leaving.

"Well" — he said — "there's five grand gone; not that I was betting on it, pal. I wonder if you would tell me something, just idle curiosity." Mr. Maddock's eyes opened wider. "Will that Jap G-man come in when the pay-off comes to-night? It's a nice-sized roll that's going."

Wilson Hitchings tried to copy Mr. Maddock's languor. He tried to show no more interest than Mr. Maddock showed.

"I don't know what you are talking about," he said, "but go ahead. I am interested."

Mr. Maddock rubbed his fingers on his coat sleeve.

"Nuts," he said. "One of the carrier pigeons is going out to-night, but then I guess you're wise. Well, I think I'll be moving. Thank you for the hot milk, pal." Mr. Maddock drew his feet beneath the chair, and prepared to rise.

"Just a minute," Wilson said. "Just a minute before you go. What was your idea in coming here, Mr. Maddock? Do you want to tell me, or shall I guess?"

Mr. Maddock rose and brushed his coat.

"You don't have to guess," he said. "I've told you,

pal, and you're not snowing, because you got my drift. I came here to see how much you knew and you know plenty. Not as much as I thought you did — but plenty. You know enough so that the spiggety crowd I'm in won't sit still and be reasonable. I told you, I won't be mixed up in a killing on an island. For you, you can suit yourself, but for me, I know when it's time to lam. I'm telling you the truth and you're wise enough to know it. Take care of yourself. I'll be seeing you sometime, pal." Mr. Maddock nodded, waved his right hand genially, and opened the door with his left and moved out sideways, while Wilson Hitchings stood in his dressing-gown, staring after him.

Even when Mr. Maddock was gone, the echo of his homely phrases seemed to remain in the room. Wilson Hitchings drew his hand across his forehead. He had never realized before that the world was made up of so many divergent personalities. He had never seen anyone less trustworthy than Mr. Maddock. Nevertheless, he was almost sure that Mr. Maddock had been telling him the truth, that there was something weighing heavily on Mr. Maddock's mind. There was no longer any doubt, also, that Mr. Moto had been telling him the truth. The Hitchings Plantation was only a façade and Eva Hitchings was only a part of that façade.

"I've got to get her out of this," Wilson Hitchings

spoke out loud. "She doesn't understand them. She can't understand."

Then it occurred to him that it would do no good for him to reason with her. He must speak to someone whose judgment she would respect. His mind turned logically to Mr. Wilkie, the Manager of Hitchings Brothers. He remembered Mr. Wilkie had said that Eva Hitchings was like his own little girl, and Mr. Wilkie was an honest man. He would talk to him that morning and Mr. Wilkie would talk to Eva Hitchings.

He was pleased with his decision, because he knew it was just the sort of thing the family would have applauded. Mr. Wilkie had been employed by Hitchings Brothers for a long while — too long, Wilson thought, for there to be the slightest doubt as to his personal integrity. No matter what his feelings toward Hitchings Plantation might have been, now that there was a possibility of the Hitchings Banking House becoming involved in an unsavory matter Mr. Wilkie would undoubtedly be loyal. Besides, he certainly did not know that Eva Hitchings might be in definite danger.

CHAPTER VIII

THERE was not the slightest doubt in Wilson Hitchings' mind that he was doing the proper thing that morning. The day was enough to confirm his opinion; the air was neither hot nor cold, the sun was out, and white clouds moved slowly across the sky keeping pace with the gentle breeze. All along the road to the city there were hedges of oleander and hibiscus, and the sea was a fine dark blue; the soft greens of the Island and the cloud haze over the tops of the mountains made a contrast against that level blueness of the sea which was restful and reassuring. The city itself had that same reassuring quality of solidity and ease. Wilson Hitchings could believe that nothing out of the ordinary could possibly happen here, in a day that was too clear and in a life that was too pleasant for undue exertion.

The offices of Hitchings Brothers had that same sort of solidity and ease. There was no undue hurry in the high, cool outer rooms, but Wilson Hitchings was pleased to see that he was known already, and he was shown at once to Mr. Wilkie's office, without any questions being asked.

Mr. Wilkie's manner was different, also. He rose and hurried around the corner of his desk, hospitably.

"Now this is a coincidence," Mr. Wilkie said. "You've been on my mind all morning, a clear case of guilty conscience. I'm afraid I wasn't — well — not very hospitable yesterday. It was the surprise of your arrival, and it was a busy day."

"Please don't be worried," Wilson said. "I imagine you have been worried, Mr. Wilkie."

"Only worried because I may have appeared casual," Mr. Wilkie said. "But I made a plan this morning. I hope you will fall in with it. I was just going to telephone you. I was about to send you a cordial invitation." Mr. Wilkie paused and smiled. "Perhaps your uncle told you that I had a seagoing boat?"

"Why yes, he did," said Wilson. He spoke politely, although it made him impatient that Mr. Wilkie's mind should have turned to yachting at such a time.

"It's a hobby of mine," said Mr. Wilkie. "I suppose a rather expensive hobby, but you might take advantage of it on a day like this. I was going to ask if you wouldn't like to take my sampan for a turn outside the harbor, and I've asked — a friend — to go with you. I've ordered lunch put aboard, in case you'd like to go. I hope you will, because it will combine business and pleasure, in a way."

Some time later in trying to recall the circumstances which surrounded that offer of Mr. Wilkie's, Wilson Hitchings could only remember with surprise the simplicity of his own reaction when he received it. He remembered that his uncle had implied that boating was an outside pleasure which perhaps took Mr. Wilkie's attention away too much from business. Mr. Wilkie's appearance that morning was too good-natured, too much like a man of leisure . . . and yet he might have been wrong. The entire atmosphere of the Island was so genial that morning that perhaps Mr. Wilkie represented something that Hitchings Brothers needed there in the way of friendliness and good will.

"Exactly what is a sampan?" Wilson asked.

Mr. Wilkie's laugh was enough to show that any pique he may have felt toward Wilson the day before had entirely evaporated.

"I forgot you were a *malihini,*" Mr. Wilkie said. "That means a newcomer to the Island, in case you don't know the word. We all get to using a bit of the Polynesian language out here. You will too, if you stay long enough, and I keep forgetting that a Hitchings doesn't know the Islands as well as I do. I was worried yesterday and you must forgive me for it. I might have known that you would be absolutely fair in dealing with Eva. But to get back to what I was saying. You don't know what a sampan is, then. It is a vessel designed by the Japanese fishing fleet here. You may have seen some on your way from the hotel. They are about as seaworthy a craft as you can find anywhere. They are used by the tuna fishers, for expeditions sometimes a thousand miles offshore. They are a sturdy type of Diesel motor craft, built along Japanese lines, with modern Diesel engines. Mine has a cruising radius of more than two thousand miles. I use my sampan for fishing and cruises about the Islands, and for moonlight picnics. I always offer visitors a trip aboard her. I hope you will say you will go." Mr. Wilkie paused. His mild brown eyes were kindly. "I hope you'll say you'll go, because I asked Eva to go with you."

Wilson Hitchings laid down his hat on the corner of Mr. Wilkie's desk and at the same time he tried to lay aside any expression of doubt or astonishment.

"I can't imagine that she accepted," he said, "but I am glad you brought her name up. I came here to talk to you about her. Do you mind if I close the door?"

Mr. Wilkie closed the door himself and sat down behind his desk.

"I am very glad of that," he said, seriously, "because I wanted to do the same thing, Hitchings. I talked to Eva seriously last night and I have been thinking of her a good deal this morning. She told me about the offer you made. I had never believed that you would make her an offer so fair and generous. Frankly, I wanted her to accept that offer and I wanted her to forget all her pique. You probably feel as I do that a gambling house is no place for Eva. It's a gesture on her part that has gone far enough. I think if she can get to know you better, if she can understand that you are perfectly sincere, she will agree to everything. That is why I suggest a few hours at lunch to-day. I know as well as you do that we must clear this matter up."

Wilson remembered something which his uncle had said in Shanghai, while Mr. Wilkie was speaking. His uncle had spoken of a connoisseur's ability to judge a picture. His uncle had said that an amateur might see nothing wrong but to an experienced observer the values might not be right. There was something wrong in the picture now. There was something wrong about Mr. Wilkie. He was betraying an excitement which was not natural. His eyes were too bright. He was laboring under some excitement beyond Wilson's knowledge but there was one thing of which Wilson was sure. For some reason of his own, Mr. Wilkie wanted him out of the way. He wanted him aboard that boat. He remembered that his uncle had spoken of Mr. Wilkie's sampan. He could not help remembering that only yesterday Mr. Wilkie had been almost hostile. He presented his last thought to Mr. Wilkie in a question which was almost blunt. As he did so, he looked at Mr. Wilkie again. There was no doubt that Mr. Wilkie was agitated — in spite of all his efforts to be casual.

"You didn't feel this way yesterday. What has made you change?" he asked.

Mr. Wilkie's face grew serious.

"Sober afterthought, if you want the truth," he said. "Eva is like my own little girl, Mr. Hitchings. I have felt her wrongs very keenly and I have felt the anomalous position in which she has been put through no fault of her own. When you came here yesterday, your assurance annoyed me; but I am over all that now. The best thing for Eva and the best thing for the firm is to have her take your offer. Eva understands it now, I think. She'll be down at the sampan in half an hour."

Wilson Hitchings listened carefully; his opinion of Mr. Wilkie was falling as he listened. It seemed to him that Mr. Wilkie was not the man to be head of the Hitchings office; that he was weak and full of contradictions.

"I am wondering," Wilson said, "just what you heard about Hitchings Plantation to make you change your mind. Have you heard anything, Mr. Wilkie?"

Mr. Wilkie opened his mouth and closed it.

"Heard about Hitchings Plantation?" he answered. "Why, what is there to hear? It's a trifle illegal, but it's conducted by the authorities, and it's very well conducted. I never go there, myself, except to see Eva now and then. I don't understand you, Hitchings. What could I have heard?"

The very vagueness of Mr. Wilkie's answer made Wilson believe him. It was the answer of a man who had allowed himself to fall into a languid rut until he had become oblivious to everything, except what went on immediately around him.

"Then you don't know who runs the gambling end of the establishment for her?" Wilson inquired.

"Why yes," Mr. Wilkie answered. "Of course I know. Eva has hired some professionals, of course. A Mr. Maddock and some others. Rather unusual types, but they are honest. What do you mean to imply, Hitchings?"

"Would it surprise you," Wilson Hitchings asked, "if I told you that I had a talk with Mr. Maddock this morning in which he told me that something so serious is going on there that he is planning to leave?"

Mr. Wilkie raised his hands and dropped them softly in front of him on the desk. "Good God!" he said. "What has been going on?"

There was such astonishment in Mr. Wilkie's voice that Wilson was almost sorry for him. There was not much further doubt in his mind that Mr. Wilkie had been very careless of the interests of the firm. There would be trouble for Wilkie when they heard of it at home.

"That's just what I am going to find out," answered Wilson Hitchings, slowly. "I'll tell you what I know. I am sure no one suspected anything like this, when my uncle sent me here. A Japanese secret service agent is watching the Plantation, Mr. Wilkie. He is watching it because there is a gang there which is using the establishment as a means of transferring money from China to revolutionaries in Manchuria. The funds are first deposited in this Branch of Hitchings Brothers, Mr. Wilkie."

Mr. Wilkie rose and leaned against the desk.

"You are not serious," he said. His speech was hoarse and uncertain. "It — it isn't possible."

"I'm afraid it is," Wilson answered steadily. He was sorry for Mr. Wilkie, but he blamed him also, for his complete carelessness and lack of observation. "I'm afraid that you and Miss Eva have been used by some rather unscrupulous persons. A Chinese, named Chang Lo-Shih, has been forwarding money here. It has been taken to Hitchings Plantation and distributed. I think I can find out exactly how, to-night, but in the meanwhile, you had better get Miss Eva out of there because it is dangerous. Also we must get the Bank cleared of all this. I hope you understand."

There was no doubt any longer that Mr. Wilkie understood, and also that it was a blow to Mr. Wilkie. The color had drained from his face, making him look old and uncertain.

"We had better call for the police," he said, hoarsely. "This must be stopped at once — at once."

"No," said Wilson, quickly. "That's exactly what we mustn't do. We mustn't get the Bank involved in any such publicity. I want to get to the bottom of this myself, because I represent the family. There mustn't be any talk until we find out how the transfer is made. I think I can find out to-night. In the meanwhile I am going to send a cable to Shanghai. Miss Hitchings must be kept out of it. I'll leave that part to you."

Mr. Wilkie squared his shoulders.

"You must talk to Eva yourself," he said. "I could swear that Eva doesn't know a thing about this. Yes, I can see. We must go on as though we know nothing. I shall go over the Chang account. I am right behind you, Hitchings."

He held out his hand and Wilson took it. "I did not think about this when I suggested the sampan, but now I think it is the very thing. If anyone is watching you, it will throw them off the track. I shall be busy here with the Chang account. Someone must find out just what Eva knows. You must do that, Mr. Hitchings, and then come back here. I will take you down to the boat myself. I am right behind you, understand? You will do that, won't you?"

Wilson Hitchings hesitated, because something in Mr. Wilkie's manner confused him even then, and it half-aroused in him an inherited sense of caution. It occurred to him again that Mr. Wilkie seemed disproportionately anxious to get him on board that sampan. It occurred to him again that Mr. Wilkie was anxious to be rid of him, although he could not tell just why The best way of finding out why might be to go aboard that boat. Mr. Wilkie seemed to read his thoughts.

"We must get things straight with Eva," Mr. Wilkie said. "That's the most important thing just now. She must not be involved in this, as you said. If she is, it will hurt the name of the firm more than anything else. I am aroused now, Hitchings, very much aroused. You must see Eva and arrange to close up Hitchings Plantation, and the sampan is the very place. No one will overhear you. There'll be lunch aboard for you and you will be back by two o'clock. Then we will attend to the rest of it and we will move fast."

Mr. Wilkie's ideas were plausible. Wilson realized that he could not have made a better opportunity to make Eva Hitchings see reason if he had tried. A good many things could be cleared up by seeing Eva

Hitchings. If he could convince her of the seriousness of the situation, a great deal might be done; and now he had his chance. More than anything else, however, he realized that he wanted to see Eva Hitchings. He wanted her to see him in a proper light. He wanted to help her in spite of her coldness to him and in spite of her disbelief in him. It did not take much intelligence to realize that matters in some way were coming to a head. Mr. Moto's manner had indicated that, and so had Mr. Maddock's. Wilson knew that the Plantation was no place for Eva Hitchings any longer.

"Are you absolutely sure that we will be back by two?" he asked.

"Absolutely." Mr. Wilkie's voice was emphatic. "There's too much to be done to have you delay any longer. I'll give all the orders."

"Are you coming too?" Wilson asked.

Mr. Wilkie shook his head.

"No," he said. "It would only complicate matters, having me along, and there is a good deal for me to do here. I must go over the Chang account. You will excuse me, won't you?"

Wilson felt relieved to hear that Mr. Wilkie was not going — without knowing exactly why, except that he preferred to see Eva Hitchings alone.

"All right," he said. "I'll go."

"Good," said Mr. Wilkie, and he took down his Panama hat from a peg. "Then we had better start at once. Come along, Eva will be waiting."

They had nearly reached the door when the telephone rang on Mr. Wilkie's desk. He turned impatiently and picked up the receiver.

"Hello," he said. "Who?"

From where he was standing, Wilson could hear the telephone making a tinny, singsong sound and he saw that Mr. Wilkie was watching him as he listened.

"Yes," Mr. Wilkie was saying. "Yes, I understand. I'll see you in a quarter of an hour. Yes, certainly, in a quarter of an hour." And he set the telephone down, slowly, and there was a tremor of excitement in his voice.

"Do you know who that was?" he said. "I couldn't have believed it; it's the very man we were speaking of. It's Mr. Chang Lo-Shih. He must have come on the same boat with you. He wants to see me right away. Don't worry. I'll see that he won't suspect anything."

"I would like to see him myself," said Wilson.

"You shall," said Mr. Wilkie. "You shall, this afternoon." And they walked through the office into the bright sun of the street. Mr. Wilkie was walking swiftly toward the waterfront. "This is serious," he said.

"Yes," said Wilson. "I think it is." And he wondered if Mr. Moto knew that Mr. Chang was there.

Mr. Wilkie rested his hand on Wilson's shoulder. "Don't you worry," Mr. Wilkie said. "I've lived in the Orient. I can attend to Chang. We will have to close out his account, right away. We've got to get clear of this. I'll close up with Chang and you manage Eva. Don't be worried, Hitchings. You will find these troubles come up every now and then. Everything will be all right."

"Yes," said Wilson. "I am sure it will." But he was not sure. In spite of Mr. Wilkie's sudden burst of energy, he felt entirely alone. He wished that his Uncle William were there, because he felt so alone.

"There is just one thing," he said. "Will you cable Shanghai, Mr. Wilkie, and tell them to close out Chang's account there?"

"Of course," said Mr. Wilkie. "Don't you worry. We have had undesirable clients before. We will have a confirmation, by the time you are back. Well, here we are."

Wilson had been so busy with his own thoughts that he had not noticed where they were going, except in a half-conscious way, until Mr. Wilkie spoke. They were standing on an open pier, looking down at the deck of a boat that was moored beside it. She was a heavily built, wide-beamed motor craft, painted blue, with an awning over the afterdeck. There was a deck cabin and an open hatch leading from the engine room, forward. The lines of the vessel were new to Wilson Hitchings. They were blunt and heavy and foreign, but she was a capable-looking craft. On the forward deck, two of the crew were standing — squat, barefoot men, with dungarees and white shirts, with bronze skins and uncertain racial traits. Eva Hitchings was seated in a canvas chair beneath the awning. When she saw them, she waved her hand.

"George," called Mr. Wilkie. "George." A snub-nosed man in a greasy hat climbed up the ladder in the hatch. He was a European and a sailor, the sort that one might see in any seaport, with strong forearms and a heavy face. He looked like a piece of driftwood that had been banged about by the sea, with scars of experience printed on his skin.

"George," said Mr. Wilkie, "this is Mr. Hitchings."

George grinned slowly and rubbed his hands on his dungarees.

"Pleased to meet you, mister," he said. His movements were slow and his face was dull and heavy. There were deep creases about his eyes and his teeth were very bad.

"George," said Mr. Wilkie, "Mr. Hitchings must be back by two o'clock. Be sure to get him back."

"Yes," said George. "Sure."

"Well," said Mr. Wilkie, "that's all. Have a good time, both of you."

Eva Hitchings stood up. "Aren't you coming with us, Uncle Joe?" she asked.

"No, my dear," said Mr. Wilkie. "Not to-day. We are very busy at the office. But George will look after you, and Kito is in the cabin to get you lunch."

Eva Hitchings frowned. "I thought you said—" she began.

But Mr. Wilkie interrupted her.

"Please, Eva," he said. "I had no idea I would be so busy this morning."

"Well, I don't like it," Eva Hitchings answered, and she gazed at Wilson coldly. "I didn't ask for this."

Wilson Hitchings was standing by the steps of the stone pier which led down to the deck. But, before he walked down them, he hesitated.

"Perhaps Miss Hitchings would like it better if I didn't go," he said.

"Nonsense," Mr. Wilkie said quickly, his lowered voice urgent. "Get aboard, this is important. You can cast off, George, but remember what I told you."

"Sure," said George. "Cast off, you!" And he disappeared down the forward hatch.

There was a sound of the starting engine, powerful and steady. One of the crew was casting off the lines. The other walked to the wheel at the stern. Their casually quick motions showed that the two hands knew their business. The sampan was moving from the dock and Mr. Wilkie waved his hat.

"Good-by," he called, and Wilson waved back, but Eva Hitchings did not move. She was standing on the deck beneath the awning, the wind was whipping her light silk skirt. Her legs were brown and bare. She was wearing a blue sweater and it seemed to Wilson that her whole dress was as casual as her manner.

"Well," she said, "now that you are here, you may as well sit down. Kito, bring a chair for Mr. Hitchings."

A Japanese boy in a white steward's uniform came out of the cabin, bringing another canvas folding armchair.

"I did not arrange this," Eva Hitchings said. "Uncle Joe asked me to have lunch with him. I hadn't the least idea that you would be connected with it."

Wilson Hitchings looked at the dock where Mr. Wilkie still stood watching. He was still puzzled by something in Mr. Wilkie's manner. The older man had been very anxious to see him safe aboard and out into the harbor. There was no doubt of that. Now that the sampan was moving out to sea, it occurred to him that Mr. Wilkie had been almost too anxious. He looked at Eva Hitchings curiously.

"Don't apologize," he said.

"I am not apologizing," she answered.

"All right," Wilson told her. "I am glad you are not. Then I won't apologize either. May I make a suggestion, now that we are here?"

"What suggestion?" Eva Hitchings asked. "Are you always so cool and calm? Do you always act as though you were addressing a directors' meeting? Doesn't anything ever stop your being so complacent?"

"As a matter of fact, I am not cool or calm at all," Wilson answered slowly. He wanted her to like him. Although he knew that his desire was unreasonable, he wished that they could be friends. "I was only going to suggest," he explained, "that we might stop quarreling for a little while. I did not plan this either, but Mr. Wilkie wanted me to talk to you."

"Don't you think you have talked to me enough? I know almost everything that is in your mind."

"Don't you think you could just treat me as a poor *malihini*?" Wilson answered. "That's the name you have for it, isn't it? I've always heard that the natives here were supposed to be hospitable. This is your boat more than mine. Couldn't we get along without quarreling?"

She smiled at him and when she smiled he knew that there was something between them, whether they admitted it or not.

189

"Do you think we could ever stop quarreling?" she asked.

"We might," said Wilson. "You never can tell until you try."

"I am afraid not," Eva said. "You and I are both rather determined people and we don't want the same thing."

"I only want to help you," Wilson said. "I have told you that."

Eva Hitchings looked at the water and back at him.

"Why?" she asked.

"Because I like you," Wilson said. "Haven't I told you that?"

"No," she said. "You haven't."

"Well," he said, "I have told you now. . . . Mr. Maddock called to see me this morning."

Her eyes grew darker and he knew that she was startled.

"He did?" she replied carelessly. "And what did Mr. Maddock want?"

"He wanted to tell me something," Wilson said. "Mr. Maddock is very much disturbed by something which he thinks may happen. He says he doesn't want to get mixed up in a killing on an island. Do you know what he means?"

Eva Hitchings shrugged her shoulders, and then her voice was appealing. "Can't we forget all this for a little while? Can't we — can't we, please? I am tired of thinking — thinking all the time. I am sick and tired of everything. I should rather like you, too, if I had met you somewhere casually, particularly if your name were not Hitchings. Kito, will you bring us some cocktails, please?"

When he tasted the cocktails, Wilson realized that Mr. Wilkie had done things very well. And everything had changed now that Eva Hitchings had spoken. They began to talk of ships and sailing. He had always been fond of the sea, as the sea had been in his blood. He felt better when they were through the opening in the reef and heading straight out over the blue water. The color of the sea inside the waves, and the fresh breeze on his face, made him forget a good deal. What interested him most was that an attractive girl was with him and that he was having a pleasant time. He never remembered exactly what they had talked about, but he knew her a good deal better before they were through.

CHAPTER IX

K ITO, the Japanese, brought them sandwiches
from the cabin, then afterwards they went forward
and sat near the bow. Nothing disturbed Wilson for a
long while until he looked at his watch. Their course
had been straight from land and they had been going
at a good rate of speed, until the Island had grown
hazy and everything upon it indistinct except for
the tones of browns and greens in the mountains.

"I never knew it was as late as this," Wilson said.
"We are going to be late getting back. We ought to
turn around."

Eva Hitchings looked back at the Island and
nodded. Wilson walked to the open hatch of the
engine room. The white man, George, was leaning
over a piece of machinery. The noise was loud enough
so that he did not notice Wilson looking down. The
man's heavy back was bent forward. There was an
indistinct bulge in his hip pocket but its outlines were
plain enough for Wilson to see that George was
carrying a gun. It was the first thing since they had

left the dock which disturbed him, the first thing which made him suspicious and alert. Wilson raised his voice above the smooth sound of the engine.

"You, down there!" he called.

George straightened up quickly at the sound of his voice and rubbed his heavy forearm across his forehead and scowled into the sunlight.

"You had better turn," Wilson called to him. "It is late."

George climbed up the ladder to the deck. Wilson did not realize how heavy and powerful the man was until he stood beside him. George was greasy and perspiring freely.

"All right, Mister," he said. "You can tell the boy at the wheel to turn her. You and the lady had better stay aft. The bow will get wet when he turns."

"Thanks," said Wilson. "I am sorry I have to go back so soon, but we are going to be late, anyway. We must be a good ten miles offshore."

"Yes," said George slowly. "About ten miles, Mister, but I will get you back all right."

The smile lingered about George's heavy lips as though something amused him.

"Yes," he repeated, slowly. "I'll get you home, Mister."

"Thank you," said Wilson. "I am sure you will." He called Eva Hitchings and they walked aft past the cabin into the cockpit beneath the awning.

"I suppose Mr. Wilkie has had George for a long time?" Wilson said.

"Yes," Eva Hitchings answered. "What makes you ask?"

"Only idle curiosity," Wilson said. But he was no longer idly curious, because certain elements of the morning were growing picturesquely and startlingly together. Mr. Wilkie's anxiety to get him aboard that boat and even Eva Hitchings' efforts to be agreeable came logically together when he thought of the man in the engine room. He moved over toward the coffee-colored, barefoot sailor by the wheel.

"You can turn now," he said. "We're going back."

The man looked at him vacantly and grinned.

"Do you want to go back now?" he asked.

"Yes," said Wilson, sharply. "George told me to tell you."

"All right," the man said. "Oh, yes, we go back." And he began to move the wheel.

As the sampan responded, they felt the full force of the rolling sea and the trade wind. The motion changed so that he had to brace himself, and then the pulsing of the engine stopped. Wilson looked at Eva Hitchings, questioningly.

"I wonder what is the matter now?" he said.

"I suppose there is something wrong with the motor," she answered.

Wilson nodded and climbed out of the cockpit.

"Where are you going?" she asked. It might have been his imagination, but it seemed to him that there was a new edge to her voice and he did not answer her. Instead, without speaking, he walked around the cabin and paused by the engine-room hatch. The second member of the crew was sitting near the bow, staring into space. The sampan had lost her way already and was rolling idly in the sea. Then Wilson climbed down the ladder quickly. The engineer was seated, doing nothing, but he rose when Wilson stepped off the ladder, and grinned.

"What is wrong?" Wilson asked. "Why have we stopped?"

The grin on George's face grew broader.

"Something wrong with the pump, Mister," George said. "It looks like we're busted down."

Wilson Hitchings tried to make his face show nothing, but his heart was beating fast. There was a rack of wrenches beside him and, as the ship rolled, he lost his balance and regained it by leaning his hand against the rack.

"Will it take a long while to fix?" he asked.

George grinned at him more openly than he had before.

"Yes," he said. "It's a tough job, Mister. I'll get you in all right, but you might as well be patient. We ain't gonna tie up to any dock until mighty late to-night."

Wilson stared at the machinery with all the stupidity of a landsman, and allowed his voice to rise.

"But I've got to get back; it's important I get back," he said.

His anxiety seemed to afford George a certain amount of quiet amusement.

"Well, you ain't going to, Mister," George said. "The engine is busted and we're going to stay right here."

Wilson stared at the machinery again.

"That's funny," he said, slowly. "Everything looks all right to me, except I saw you fiddling with that pump when I called you five minutes ago. Who told you to fiddle with it? Was it Mr. Wilkie, George?"

It was clear that deception was not in George's line. His face was enough to show Wilson that he was absolutely right. The answer was written in the flicker of George's eyelids. A good two seconds before he spoke Wilson knew as sure as fate that it was Mr. Wilkie who had put him on that boat and it was Mr. Wilkie's intention that he should stay there. As he watched George struggling with the mental problem which confronted him, Wilson knew that he must do something very quickly, before George thought ahead too far.

It was amazing how quickly and eccentrically his mind ran in that brief lapse of time, before that slow-witted man could speak. He felt, with all the sharp shock of surprise, incredulity that Mr. Wilkie should be playing any part in such an affair as that. But it all was perfectly clear as he stood in the oily engine room. He tried to restrain his anger and think. The man in front of him was more than a match for him physically, and Wilson knew that George knew it, and was ready to use his strength. Wilson knew that he must do something very quickly, something which he had never done in his life before; but he had already pictured the whole act in his mind. His hand was resting on a wrench. It was loose beneath his hand in the rack and George was speaking.

"What if he did?" George said. "It ain't my business, Mister."

"No," said Wilson, slowly. "It's not your business, George."

He intended his next move to be unexpected, and it was. He had pulled the wrench gently out of the rack as he was speaking, and he swung it in a sharp sidewise blow that caught George behind the ear. The result was more than he had anticipated, although he had been careful not to strike too hard. The sailor's mouth sagged. His eyes glazed and his knees buckled. He sank in a heap at Wilson's feet and sprawled on the grating beside the engine, while Wilson stood looking at him, half amazed, half shocked at himself, still holding the wrench in his right hand. At first he had a sickening thought that he had killed the man, but he saw it was not so a moment later when he stooped and felt behind the greasy hair where he had struck. He had not broken the skull, but the man was knocked out cold. What surprised Wilson most was that he felt no perturbation or panic after that first sickening moment. Instead he could almost have believed that he had been used to such actions all his life.

He seemed to know exactly what to do. First he reached into the hip pocket of the figure that lay sprawled before him, then drew out a gunmetal revolver and placed it in his own pocket. Then he felt in the side pocket and pulled out a knife. There was a coil of light rope lying by the ladder. He cut two lengths of it quickly, and tied the man's hands and feet. Then he took the rest of the coil and climbed out of the engine room to the deck. Everything was exactly as he had left it. The ship still rolled in the trough of the sea. He could see the helmsman gazing at him over the top of the cabin. The second man still sat in the bow. Wilson called to him.

"You there," he called, "George wants you."

The man moved toward him slowly, without the least suspicion that anything was wrong. He did not notice that anything was amiss until he was down the ladder and in the engine room, and then he had no chance to make a sound, because Wilson told him not to, with a revolver in his hand, just as though he had done such things always.

"You don't want to get sick like George, do you?" he said. "Then lie down on your face and don't make any noise. I am going to tie you up, boy."

Three minutes later, Wilson walked aft, still holding the revolver.

"Stand still, you," he said to the man at the wheel. "Stand exactly where you are!"

Eva Hitchings was staring at him, open-mouthed.

"What is it?" she cried. "Have you gone crazy?"

Wilson Hitchings shook his head.

"There seems to be a little trouble here," he answered. "You said I was a cool customer and I begin to believe you are right. I have tied two men up and now I am going to tie up this one. Will you go into the cabin, please, and stay there until I call you?"

"No," she said. "I won't."

"I am afraid you will," Wilson answered, "unless you want me to pick you up and toss you in there. Go into the cabin and stay with the steward."

He did not think she would do what he ordered, but she did. She turned away without a word, and he slammed the cabin door behind her.

Ten minutes later, Wilson Hitchings pulled out the piece of iron which he had inserted in the hasp of the cabin door. He had removed his coat and rolled up his sleeves, for he was hot from unaccustomed exertion.

"Kito," he said, "you come out here!"

The Japanese steward came out slowly, holding his hands above his head.

"Please, sir?" he began. "Please?"

"Put down your hands!" Wilson told him. "Are you going to be a good boy, Kito?"

"Yes," said Kito. "Oh, yes. I do not understand."

"There is only one thing you need to understand," said Wilson. "I am in charge of this boat now, Kito. You behave, and I won't hurt you. Stay in the cabin, unless I call you. If you try to sneak forward, I will wring your neck."

"Yes," said Kito. "Oh, yes, sir."

"And now," Wilson said, "you tell the missy, I want her to come out and talk to me. You tell her to come out quick."

Wilson stood with his feet apart and his hands on his hips, swaying with the rhythm of the drifting sampan. He could not believe he was the same person he had known all his life: a quiet, well-mannered, conventional person, both repressed and shy. He was still half-stunned by his own capacities, which had been revealed by what he had done in those last few minutes. He wondered if a criminal felt as he did on achieving his first deed of violence; whether his surprise was the same. He had heard of the subconscious mind and of the unexpected capabilities of persons laboring under great excitement. He could almost believe that he was a psychological case, a dual personality. He still could not exactly believe all he had done and yet some voice inside him prompted him to go ahead. He felt a curious mixture of disillusion and of anger. It seemed to him that he had never known, until then, any real emotion, hot and strong, that could galvanize the nerves into sudden action and could tear away inhibitions and manners.

When he saw Eva Hitchings walking toward him, everything that he had thought about her, and every wishful illusion that had warped his opinion of her from reality to some sort of mawkish romance, was gone into ashes like a sheet of paper that strikes a bed of white-hot coals. It seemed to him that he saw her at last entirely accurately, just as Mr. Moto saw her. He could hear Mr. Moto saying, "I am afraid she is not nice. I am very, very sorry."

Eva Hitchings must have seen what he was thinking, because her face was assuming a startled look. First she had looked as though she were about to demand an explanation but now she was obviously startled.

"What is it?" she asked. Her voice was timid. "What has come over you, Wilson Hitchings?"

She was acting still, and he wanted her to know that he knew it.

"I guess it's common sense, Eva," he told her; "common sense has come over me for the first time in my life. I should have known what you are and what your friend Mr. Wilkie is, if you had not been so pretty, Eva Hitchings. You are both of you a pair of crooks, using the Hitchings Bank in your schemes. But when you thought I knew too much, you thought you could get me out here, while you cleaned up your game. You wanted me out of the way and you thought I would believe some story about a broken engine, while your Uncle Joe — isn't that what you call him? — cleaned up his business with Mr. Chang from Shanghai. Didn't you, Eva Hitchings? Well, you made just one mistake. I happen to know a good deal about boats and Diesel power. There is nothing wrong with that engine that I can't fix up in five minutes. I saw your seagoing friend George throwing it out of whack."

"But what did you do?" she asked. "I don't see how you could have . . ."

Wilson laughed at her and she did not finish her question.

"It surprises you, does it?" he inquired. "Well, I guess the Hitchingses are a tough lot, Eva. It probably runs in the family. I was a little surprised myself, but I am getting used to it now. I will tell you something else, Eva, that perhaps you did not know. I am perfectly able to start that engine and to bring this boat in by myself and I am going to do it. Now I think you had better go into the cabin again, unless there is something you want particularly to say."

Eva Hitchings did not move. Her eyes met his and the trade wind blew her hair across her forehead.

"I don't believe a word of it, not a single word."

Wilson shrugged his shoulders.

"It doesn't really make much difference what you believe," he said. "The Hawaiians have a word for it. Your friend Mr. Maddock told it to me, this morning. You are through, Eva Hitchings, and the word for it is *pau*. I like that word. You and your gang of crooks are very nearly *pau*. I offered to buy your place last night, but now I am going to save the money. You are going to be put out with your gunmen, Eva."

Eva Hitchings moved convulsively, as though something invisible were clutching at her throat.

"It isn't so!" she cried. Her voice was strained and discordant. "It isn't so!"

"It won't do any good to act that way," Wilson told her. "If you are going to have hysterics, have them in the cabin."

Eva Hitchings pushed her hair back from her forehead.

"I won't have any," she said. "I would not give you the satisfaction; but I repeat, it isn't so."

In spite of himself, Wilson looked at her admiringly.

"No, Eva, it won't do," he said. "Who came last night to see if Mr. Moto had taken his drink of whisky? Your friend, Mr. Wilkie, came. I thought it was coincidence, until he got me aboard this boat."

Eva Hitchings opened her lips and closed them, as though something stopped her from speaking.

"I don't believe it. I can't believe it."

"Well," said Wilson, "that's your own affair."

"I don't care about myself," she continued, as though she had not heard him. "They — they bought me out six months ago, with an agreement that I should stay on for a year, so that no one should know about it. Uncle Joe arranged it, but he wouldn't do a thing like that."

"Wouldn't he?" Wilson asked politely. He was interested in spite of himself, although he was not entirely sure that he believed her. "So you don't own Hitchings Plantation?"

Eva Hitchings shook her head.

"No, I don't," she repeated. "But I was glad to pretend I did. I told you last night that I wanted to find out what they were doing. I thought, of course, that your family was in it. Uncle Joe as good as told me they were in it. I wanted to find out exactly what they were doing. I have never liked your family."

"And you thought I was in it?" Wilson Hitchings asked.

"Yes, of course, I did," Eva Hitchings answered. "But I don't think so now."

"Would you mind telling me why you don't?" Wilson asked her. And her answer was logical enough.

"Because you wouldn't do what you have done," she said. "You wouldn't start tearing this boat apart." She looked at him steadily. "I still don't see how you did it. You haven't killed anybody, Wilson Hitchings?"

"I haven't yet," Wilson told her. "I think you tend to overestimate my capacities. I have thought so, all along."

Then he began to believe that he should never have allowed her to talk, because the ideas which he had formed about her and which he thought he had entirely eliminated were returning to him again, making his judgment fallible. When she turned her head, the curve of her neck interested him — and her change of expression when she spoke, making him forget the actual elements of the problem.

"No, I don't think I overestimated you," she answered. "I said that you were very capable and I certainly think you are, but you have overestimated me. I haven't enough capacity to be a good adventuress. Sometimes I've wished I had, but I haven't. I have just been caught in something which I haven't been able to control. I imagine you have been caught in the same thing. We are really babes in the wood and we think that we are tigers. I guess we are both wrong."

Wilson found himself repressing a strong desire to laugh.

"Are you trying to convey the idea," he inquired, "that you are a nice girl that has been led into bad company and is still at heart a thoroughly nice girl?"

Eva Hitchings nodded.

"Yes, that is roughly what I am trying to convey," she said; "but I don't suppose you believe me."

"No," said Wilson. "I don't suppose I do."

"Then, what are you going to do about it?" Eva Hitchings asked.

"I am going to put you back in the cabin," Wilson answered, "and then I am going to get the engine started. If you are so anxious to keep me out here, it must be interesting on shore."

"And you still think I had something to do with it?" Eva Hitchings asked.

"Yes," said Wilson. "Of course I do."

She gave no sign of being hurt by his disbelief, instead she seemed almost pleased.

"You were right about what you said when I first met you," she told him. "You told me you were a guileless person. I really think you are. Hasn't it ever occurred to you that I might be here for just the same reason you are — because I know too much? I hadn't thought of it that way until a few minutes ago; but it is the reason. We are both of us here because we know too much."

The drifting boat and the sounds of the sea made her words surprisingly simple. If he could believe her, everything seemed clear, and he could very nearly believe her.

"Then what are you going to do about it?" Wilson asked.

Eva Hitchings shrugged her shoulder.

"I don't know," she said, "unless you have some suggestion."

He did not understand her. He could only wonder where her thoughts might lead him next.

"Well," he replied, "I haven't any suggestion."

She looked back at him steadily.

"You don't seem to do much about using your opportunity," she said. "You said you liked me a little while ago."

"Yes," Wilson nodded, "a little while ago."

"And you don't now," Eva Hitchings asked him. "That's the way things go, isn't it? You don't like me any more. I don't suppose you trust me and now I have just begun to like you. I like you better than anyone I know."

"I am sorry I don't follow you," Wilson Hitchings said. His voice was cool enough but his thoughts were not. He was standing closer to her than he thought. She was looking up at him, brushing her hair from her forehead, and she seemed very young just then, transparently a young person.

"I don't exactly follow myself," he heard her say. And then she smiled. "I suppose it's because I am thinking about the Hitchings family."

He must have been more interested in her than he believed because he heard no sound behind him until he heard a voice and he saw Eva Hitchings start and saw her eyes grow wide and incredulous.

"Excuse me," someone said behind him. "I'm sorry that I interrupt, so very, very sorry."

Wilson Hitchings had turned as quickly as though someone had touched his back. The door of the cabin was open and Mr. Moto, blinking in the sunlight, was looking through the opening.

CHAPTER X

WILSON HITCHINGS rubbed the back of his hand across his eyes. Mr. Moto was still standing looking through the cabin door. There was no mistaking the shoebrush cut of his hair and the gold fillings in his teeth or the delicate hands or the nervous determined smile. Mr. Moto was dressed in a dark alpaca suit that was somewhat wrinkled and there were smudges of dust on his coat which he was brushing off carefully when he stepped into the cockpit.

"Excuse me," Mr. Moto said again. "I could not help but overhear. It was so very, very interesting what Miss Hitchings said, that you are both here because you know too much. And so very, very true. It is also a very good joke. That is why we are all here — because all of us know too much. Excuse me, I did not mean to startle you. Have I startled you, Mr. Hitchings?"

Wilson sat down at the edge of the cockpit.

"You did in a way," he said. "I suppose you could

imagine my next question. Did Mr. Wilkie ask you to come with us, Mr. Moto?"

Mr. Moto smiled patiently but his smile appeared to be more genuine, and Wilson thought he could detect a gleam of amusement in Mr. Moto's dark birdlike eyes.

"No, he did not ask me," Mr. Moto said. "This was purely my own idea. Please, do not look so nervous, Mr. Hitchings. I do not wish to have you nervous, because that might be very bad for me. Please, I did not know you could be so violent, Mr. Hitchings."

Then Eva Hitchings spoke.

"But where have you been?" she asked. "How did you get here? I didn't see you in the cabin, Mr. Moto."

Mr. Moto laughed. It was apparent that he was pleased and amused by the entire episode, with an almost childlike amusement.

"I will tell you," said Mr. Moto, rubbing his hands and smiling. "There is a passage forward, connecting with the engine and the crew's quarters. There is a small corridor leading from the passage. It was confined in there and not very nice. Your steward, Kito, introduced me to it. Please," Mr. Moto raised his hands decoratively, "do not interrupt me, Mr. Hitchings. I should be very, very frank. The cabin boy, Kito, is very nice. I have known his family in Japan. Please, it is this way, Mr. Hitchings. This vessel has interested me very much for several days.

It is such a well-found vessel and so very, very sea-worthy. It has interested me why Mr. Wilkie should desire such a vessel for ocean trips. There is a certain cargo steamer which touches here and then makes for Fusan in Korea. Do you understand me, Mr. Hitchings?"

"No," said Wilson, "but I am trying to, Mr. Moto."

"Ha-ha," said Mr. Moto. "That is very good. You are going to understand. Everything will be very nice, I think. The name of the steamer is the *Eastern Light,* carrying lumber from your West Coast, Mr. Hitchings. Several hours after she leaves harbor, I found this sampan leaves also. She meets the *Eastern Light* out of sight of land. Now what do you think of that?"

"I think it is very, very interesting," Wilson said.

"Thank you," said Mr. Moto. "I am very glad you think so. There is a passenger on the sampan who boards the *Eastern Light.* I have been very interested to find out just why. It must be because he does not wish to be seen walking up the gangplank. Do you not think so, Mr. Hitchings? Now there is something else which is very, very interesting. The *Eastern Light* is sailing this afternoon." Mr. Moto rubbed his hands. "This morning the sampan filled her fuel tank. I was very, very interested and then this morning Kito told me something else. It was so very, very nice that I should know him, don't you think?"

"Yes," said Wilson Hitchings. "Very, very nice."
Mr. Moto cocked his head to one side.

"Please," he continued, "would you like to guess what Kito told me? Your mind is so very, very quick that possibly you could guess."

"Possibly," Wilson agreed, "but I'd rather you told me, Mr. Moto, and if you don't mind, tell me quickly! I want to get the engine going."

"Yes," said Mr. Moto. "That will be very, very nice. I should be so glad to help you, Mr. Hitchings. This morning Mr. Wilkie hurried to the dock and gave orders that you and Miss Hitchings were going out for a little sail. He asked especially for the engine to break down so that you would not get ashore until twelve o'clock to-night, after which he wished everything ready to put to sea again. Please, when I heard of this, it made me think of several things. It made me think that I would be very much safer with you and Miss Hitchings on the sampan than any place on shore. I want to be safe, very much indeed, until to-night. Also I was worried about you, Mr. Hitchings. When I heard you in the engine-room I nearly interfered. I did not think that you would do everything so very, very nicely."

"Thank you for saying so," Wilson Hitchings said.

"You are so very welcome," answered Mr. Moto. "Please I did not know that you understood the small boats."

"Do you?" Wilson asked.

"Oh, yes," said Mr. Moto. "Please. I was in the Navy once."

"Well then, let's get the engine going," Wilson said. "I want to get ashore."

"Please," Mr. Moto raised his hand. "If I may make a suggestion . . . If I may be so very rude . . . The engine will start very easily, but I do not think it will be nice to go ashore until the sun goes down. Please, do you understand me? Someone is surely watching us from shore, right now. They will be so very, very glad to see us rolling here. I think it would be very nice if no one should know exactly when we land. There will be time after dark, I think. I hope you understand me, Mr. Hitchings."

"Yes," said Wilson, "I think I understand you."

"Then please," said Mr. Moto, "I think it would be very nice to go forward and see that everything is secure in the crew's quarters, and then perhaps it would be very nice if Kito were to give us a little refreshment. I am so glad that everything is going so beautifully. There is only one thing more."

"What's that?" Wilson asked him. But it seemed to him that there were a good many other things more.

Mr. Moto bowed toward Eva Hitchings.

"It is about Miss Hitchings," he replied. "I said some things about her which were not very nice and

213

I am afraid that you believed them, Mr. Hitchings. Excuse me. I was very, very wrong. You must believe what she tells you, because I think she will be very nice now. I think we will all be very nice and now perhaps we had better go forward, Mr. Hitchings. There is a question I should like to ask the crew."

Little as Wilson Hitchings understood the Oriental mind, it was evident that something had happened which gave Mr. Moto both relief and pleasure. For a while at any rate, a proportion of his tenseness and his eagerness had left him. He hummed a tune softly, as he examined the engines.

"You are pleased," said Wilson, "aren't you, Mr. Moto?"

"Yes," said Mr. Moto. "Very, very pleased. I have learned several things. Matters will go nicely now, I think. I simply need to set eyes on several persons. I simply need to make an observation. Then, everything will be arranged."

Mr. Moto paused and began to laugh again.

"Excuse me," he said. "I was simply thinking of certain persons who would be very, very sorry not to see me back on shore. They will be looking for me so very hard. They will be so very anxious to have me put out of the way, I think. Yes, I should like to see their faces. They will be so much annoyed. And now, please, shall we see the fellows you have tied? I wish to ask a question."

There were four bunks in the crew's quarters in the bow. George and his two helpers lay bound in the bunks where Wilson Hitchings had tossed them, and their positions indicated that they had all been struggling with their ropes. The engineer raised his head and scowled.

"Say," he said, "what the hell is the big idea? I'll get you for this, Mister." His glance moved to Mr. Moto ominously. "And that little monkey with you too. You can't get away with this, Mister."

For almost the first time that Wilson had known him, Mr. Moto looked annoyed.

"Please," he said, "what did you call me, please?"

"A monkey," said George. "I seen you snooping on the dock and I say you can't get away with this."

"Excuse me," said Mr. Moto. "I should look at the knots, I think. I mean no criticism, Mr. Hitchings, but it takes training to tie a man securely. I may be more expert, please."

Wilson was almost inclined to take the criticism to heart, for he felt that he had done his tying rather well. The only light in the small sleeping space came from a skylight on the deck and the light fell dimly on the heavy recumbent figure of the engineer as he lay on his side in the lower bunk. Mr. Moto was bending over him and Wilson was watching almost idly, when he saw something suspiciously intent in the large man's glance. He was looking over Mr.

Moto's shoulder, directly into Wilson's face, and his eyes were growing narrow.

"Ah," Mr. Moto was saying. "Exactly as I feared. The arms are very greasy and the rope — "

"Look out!" said Wilson suddenly. But Mr. Moto was not quick enough. In the half-light Wilson saw that something was very wrong. George was free of his ropes.

"Look out!" Wilson called. But Mr. Moto was not quick enough. From the semi-obscurity of the bunk George delivered a sharp, decisive blow on Mr. Moto's jaw, and Mr. Moto staggered backwards and sat down. In the same instant, George had rolled out of his bunk, landing on his feet on the deck.

"Pile on him, boys," he shouted. "We've been waiting for you, mister."

Wilson sprang backwards instinctively, and as he did so, the man who was lying on the upper bunk hurled himself on his back. The impact threw Wilson forward and nearly made him lose his balance. He always said the thing that happened next was luck. The deck hand who leaped for his back slid over him and sprawled into George's stomach and the two landed in a heap. The next instant was like the click of a camera shot. The two men were in a heap trying to get up. Mr. Moto was already on his feet, the third man was half out of his bunk.

"Get back in there!" said Wilson and, still half

doubled over, he whirled on his heels and struck the man on the face. As he did so, he heard a scream of agony. George was sitting on the deck holding his left arm. The other man was struggling to his feet, standing undecided, and Wilson moved toward him; but as he did so, he saw that the trouble was over.

"All right, sir," the man said. "I won't make no trouble, sir."

"Then get up there and lie down," Wilson Hitchings told him.

"Please," Mr. Moto was saying. "Fetch some more rope, Mr. Hitchings. I can handle everything very nicely, please."

There was no doubt that Mr. Moto was amazingly adroit. Wilson watched him with deep interest as he worked and Mr. Moto conversed quite cheerfully.

"Please, Mr. Hitchings," he said. "It was my fault as much as yours not to think of this before. I should have known they might work loose. They were waiting, of course, for you to come here. They did not wish to show themselves because you had a weapon. I am sorry that I broke the man's arm but he was not very nice. Please, Mr. Hitchings, it only shows how careful one must be. But all this is really nothing." Mr. Moto leaned over George again and felt his arm.

"Now," he said, "perhaps you will answer a question, please. It is what I came for, in the first place, please. I am sorry I shall hurt you if you do not answer. You were to bring out a passenger, a man, to the *Eastern Light* this evening. What does he look like, please?"

George groaned but did not answer.

"Quickly, please," said Mr. Moto. "I do not wish to hurt you."

"Take him away from me," George shouted. "Please, Mister, take him away."

"What does the man look like?" Mr. Moto repeated softly. He was holding a small photograph before the sailor's face. "Please — is that the man?"

"I don't know," George gasped. "I ain't never seen his face. He keeps it hid. I tell you that's the truth. He comes on with money from the Hitchings gambling house and we put him aboard the hooker, but I ain't seen his face."

"Thank you," said Mr. Moto. "Are you sure? I am very, very sorry. Answer me another question, please. I do not wish to hurt you. This man, are you going to take him out to-night?"

"Yes," said George. "He's going out to-night. Now will you take your hands off me? I don't know any more. I'm just obeying orders."

"Thank you," said Mr. Moto. "And the money comes from the gambling house? I thought so. Thank you very much."

"Wait a minute," said Wilson. "I've got a question

too. Does Mr. Wilkie bring this man down to his boat?"

George looked sick and pale. He looked so badly that Wilson was very sorry for him.

"You had better tell me, George," he said, "and I'll give you a shot of whisky. I don't like this business any more than you." George's heavy eyes moved toward him.

"I wish I had set you down for a tough guy — when I seen you," George said. "Sure Mr. Wilkie takes him down. It's his boat, ain't it? Me — I'm just obeying orders." Mr. Moto straightened up, drew a handkerchief from his pocket, and wiped his hands.

"I am so very, very sorry," he said. "I do not like putting subjects to the question. It is a method with which I know you do not sympathize but in this case it is important. It is so very, very kind of you to be so broad-minded, Mr. Hitchings. I think now we can leave this place. They will not make more trouble. I very seldom drink but I think we might all have something now. It will be so very, very nice. I shall find who the man is when we get ashore. If you will excuse me, I shall join you in a few moments. I wish to look at the engines again. One must be so very, very careful."

CHAPTER XI

Eva HITCHINGS was sitting aft by the wheel
looking across the sparkling, restless water across
the sea toward the Island. It was late afternoon and
clear and beautiful, but the clouds of the mountains
in the distance and the moisture in the air cast a faint
enigmatic haze over the Island and passing clouds
darkened the mountain slopes with shifting shadows.
Even then Wilson had time to think that the Island
was beautiful, although its soft coloring and its partial absence of definition were as disturbing as his
thoughts. No matter what Mr. Moto might do,
Wilson was thinking that he must deal with his own
affairs.

There was no doubt any longer that Mr. Wilkie had
been using his connection with the House of Hitchings in such a way that the Hitchings reputation was
in danger. Wilson had been taught that the reputation of their house was something to be guarded
even more carefully than individual honor. A breath
of scandal might blight it. No matter what happened

the family bank must not be involved. And yet, he could think of no way to stop it. There would be an open scandal, if Mr. Moto were to expose half of what he knew and Mr. Moto would surely do it, if it were to help his interests, and Wilson could not blame him.

There must have been such thoughts which had been in back of his mind all the while and now they were bearing on him heavily in his reaction from excitement. He had forgotten that he was not a free agent and now he remembered that he was not free — that he was tied hard and fast to family. For the moment he almost hated his family with all its pedantic ramifications; but even so, he knew he was a part of it, a part of it through the simplest laws of inheritance. What was worse, no one to whom he could appeal would understand his position.

Surely, Eva Hitchings would not understand it, and if she did she would only be amused, simply because she had reason to dislike the family, rather cogent reason. She turned when she heard his step and her eyes gave him the startling idea that she had been crying, although he was not entirely sure.

"Where is Mr. Moto?" she asked. "Has anything gone wrong?"

Wilson shook his head.

"Mr. Moto is examining the engine," he answered. "There was trouble with the crew."

"You don't look very happy," Eva Hitchings said.

"Neither do you," Wilson told her. Her face looked drawn and tired.

"Why should I be?" she asked. "It isn't nice to be disillusioned. It isn't pleasant to know that someone who has been kind to you is entirely different from what you thought he was. I am feeling rather sick if you want to know, sick and tired of everything. I know what you must think of me and I can't blame you much. I know what everyone will think by the time this thing is finished. I used to think that I could be independent, and now I am a part of a rotten world. It didn't used to be rotten when Father was alive. I don't suppose you believe me, do you?"

Although he did not answer, he was surprised that he did believe her, because she was not asking anything of him and because her loneliness appealed to his own loneliness.

"So you agree with me about Mr. Wilkie now?" he said. "I know the way you feel. It isn't very nice."

"No," she answered, "it isn't very nice. You are probably right about what you said a while ago. I won't have much reputation in a day or two. I'll be out in the streets with the gunmen, I suppose."

There seemed to be no reason not to be frank, since she probably understood the situation just as well as he.

"There is one thing that may console you," Wilson said. "The family won't have much reputation either. This business is too ugly for pieces of it not to come out. If the name of our firm is mentioned in it, it will be almost enough to spoil us. It doesn't take much to hurt a bank. You will probably only have to say a few words, Eva, and you will have your wish. You will get back at the family for everything they've done to you and more. That ought to console you, don't you think?"

Eva Hitchings looked surprised — genuinely surprised.

"You think I would be such a cad as that?" she said.

"Why not?" said Wilson. "You told me yesterday that was what you proposed to do. I thought that I might stop you but I don't think so now. If I did, I wouldn't be speaking as I am."

Eva Hitchings was looking at him incredulously.

"You really think I am such a cad as that?" she repeated. "Yesterday I thought your precious family was engaged in this whole business, because Mr. Wilkie told me so, and now I know they are not. I don't tell lies. The Hitchingses are decent people even if I don't like them. I am afraid I don't know many decent people."

Wilson moved toward her, surprised that all his resentment was gone.

"Do you mean that?" he asked her, quickly. "Do you mean that about the family?"

"Yes," she said. "You are part of it, aren't you? You are the only part I have ever seen. Except my father."

There was no doubt that she was telling the truth then — that she had always told the truth; and vaguely she was part of the family. Without actually knowing that he was going to do it, Wilson took her hand.

"It might be better if you told me what you know," he said.

She did not draw her hand away.

"Yes," she said. "I'll tell you."

"Thanks," said Wilson, quickly. "Now quickly, before Mr. Moto gets here, — I don't know what's keeping him, but thank Heaven he is taking his time, — tell me what you know about this. The money is deposited in the Hitchings Bank. It is drawn out and brought to Hitchings Plantation. Then someone gets on this sampan and catches a vessel out at sea. What happens at the Plantation, Eva?"

Her fingers closed on his more tightly.

"You almost guessed," she said. "You would have guessed in a little while. They bring the money up a little at a time. It is lost across the table to certain persons or the house. You guessed it was a crooked wheel and I have guessed it too. Three or four win

224

the money but it never goes out of the house. It's put in the safe. Then once in so often the same man comes, a dark man, a Russian, I think, and he wins more one night. Then he takes all the money in the safe and goes away. I never knew about the boat. I just knew about the crooked wheel and the money being lost."

Wilson thought for a moment and everything was very clear.

"That ties it," he said. "We've got the story now. Is a lot of money lost, Eva?"

"Yes," she said. "A lot over a period of weeks, but gradually. I didn't notice it at first because the house gets a profit just the same. The house is paid, whether it wins or loses. That's what I noticed first."

"And the money goes out to-night?" Wilson said.

"Yes," said Eva Hitchings. "It seems that way. A lot of money."

"All right," said Wilson. "That's the story. I wish I had known it sooner. Listen to me, Eva. The money must go out to-night. There mustn't be any trouble. Mr. Moto mustn't make any trouble. Do you understand?"

"No," she said. "I don't. I thought you wanted to stop it. Of course, I don't understand."

"Don't you see?" Wilson's voice was urgent because he saw it perfectly. "The money must go out and there will be no trouble. Everything can be arranged quietly once the money is out. If there is no hitch, there will be no scandal — nothing. I can arrange with Mr. Wilkie after that. I wish to Heaven they had told me, but I suppose they didn't think I knew so much. It's the Bank I am thinking about — the family. I don't care a tinker's damn about their money. Let the bandits have it in Manchuria as long as no one hears about it. It isn't a matter for the police, you understand. If Mr. Moto learns any more, he can say enough to ruin the Bank and I don't trust him, Eva. And you come in it too. No one will know that you are involved in this, if the money goes out to-night. Don't you see? Do you know what I am going to do?"

"No," she answered. "What?"

Wilson Hitchings drew in his breath.

"I don't like it, but I am going to do it. As soon as we get ashore, we are going to the Plantation. I am going to see Mr. Wilkie, or whoever is running this and I think I know who it is. At any rate, I am going to warn them how much Mr. Moto knows. I don't like it because Mr. Moto has taken me into his confidence. At the same time, it might very well save his life. They tried to shoot him last night and then they tried to poison him. They'll leave him alone now. They'll be too anxious to get that money away before they catch him. Mr. Moto is not going to get hurt. No one will get hurt. When it is all over, Mr. Moto can stop the money from going into Manchuria. I can save Mr. Moto's face, as they say in China. Do you see what I mean?"

"You mean you are not going to hurt anybody?" Eva Hitchings said.

"Yes, that's just what I mean," Wilson Hitchings told her. "Not Moto — I like Moto; not even Mr. Wilkie — as long as the Bank is out of this. It's the only possible thing I can do and the best for everybody. I am thinking of the family."

"Are you always thinking of the family?" Eva Hitchings asked.

"Almost always," Wilson said. "But I am thinking of you too."

Eva Hitchings smiled faintly. But not too anxiously, she said, "I'm not as delicate as a bank."

"Yes," said Wilson Hitchings. "I suppose that is true."

The smile on her lips grew broader and her eyes were mocking.

"You are not very gallant, are you?" she said. "When it comes to Hitchings Brothers, you haven't got much sense of humor."

At first Wilson did not understand why she had taken his statement personally. The family banking house was too nearly a part of himself for him to be patient when it was treated lightly. He wanted to explain to her that a bank's reputation was at the

227

present day, at any rate, more fragile than a woman's. In the disastrous years of the depression, he had seen how rumor could destroy faith. If a rumor should gain credence that Hitchings Brothers, even indirectly, had been engaged in financing dubious political groups, the whole credit of the firm would fall into disrepute, particularly when financial competition was growing heavy in the East.

"You are right," he admitted. "I have no sense of humor when it comes to Hitchings Brothers. I don't suppose I have much, at any rate. But when you are brought up in a certain mold, you can't laugh about that mold. I wish you could understand how serious this is. Japan is gaining a very strong commercial hold in the East. Japanese financiers who are competing against us would give a good deal to hear how Hitchings Brothers are involved. Mr. Moto is a Japanese. We can't hope that he'll be quiet — "

She must have been impressed by something he had said, for she was entirely serious again.

"You mean you would allow yourself to be implicated in this mess, to help the family?" she asked.

Wilson Hitchings sighed and nodded.

"I hate it worse than poison," he agreed. "I hate being in this thing. I hate having you in it. The only thing that anyone can do is to rely on his best judgment. This seems to me the best way out, that's all."

228

"You don't think much about yourself, do you?" she asked.

"No," Wilson Hitchings said. "I haven't had much time."

Eva Hitchings moved her shoulders impatiently. Her eyes as she looked at him were wide and dark.

"I wonder if you will ever have time to think about yourself," she said. "I wonder if you will ever have the time really to be yourself. You're not so attractive when you are part of a machine. I wish I could get you away from it. I like you when you forget. What would you do right now, if you and I were ordinary people? If we were just out here looking at the sea? If there wasn't any family?"

Wilson Hitchings looked back at her, and in spite of himself the idea amused him.

"If there wasn't any family," he said, "if you weren't the hostess at the Hitchings Plantation, I'd tell you that you are one of the prettiest girls I had ever seen. I might even go as far as to say, probably incorrectly, that you are one of the nicest girls that I have ever known. I'd probably be quite foolish about you because I wouldn't have to think. I'd ask you to give me as much time as possible while I was staying here. I should ask you to have dinner with me to-night. I might even ask you to come back to Shanghai. I should tell you quite irrationally that you are the sort of person I have always been looking for.

You are in a way, although I don't know exactly why."

"I should certainly change you," Eva Hitchings said. "You wouldn't know yourself when I got through with you. You wouldn't know yourself even in the mirror."

"Well, I don't suppose I should mind very much," Wilson Hitchings said. "Naturally I would try to change you too."

"I shouldn't mind either," Eva Hitchings answered, "but what would your family say?" Wilson Hitchings began to laugh and the shadows left his mind.

"I imagine they would say a good deal," he answered. The idea was new and it interested him. "I imagine they would be very much surprised." Then Eva Hitchings was laughing too.

"You're nicer now," she said.

"Be careful!" Wilson told her. "Here comes Mr. Moto. Eva, you won't let me down?" Her hand closed over his.

"No," she whispered. "I won't let you down. . . . Why, Mr. Moto, where have you been?"

Mr. Moto rubbed his hands together.

"I have been telling the boy to bring us some whisky and soda," he said. "It will be so very refreshing, don't you think so? There is a coolness on the water when the sun drops and the sun drops in these latitudes so very, very fast."

Mr. Moto was imperturbable and smiling and Wilson could not tell what Mr. Moto thought. He even had a moment's suspicion that Mr. Moto had deliberately left him alone with Eva Hitchings.

Kito had come from the cabin bringing a tray and glasses.

"Here's looking at you," Mr. Moto said. "It is so very nice the way you say it in America. But I do not know what it means."

"Neither do I," Wilson said, and he looked at Mr. Moto over the rim of his glass.

"But even so," said Mr. Moto, "the expression is very, very nice and the day is very, very nice like a painting upon silk. Do you know our Japanese artists? I think we have had some of the greatest painters in the world."

As though nothing else were on his mind, Mr. Moto seated himself and began discoursing on the culture of Japan. He seemed lost in the subject, as he sat there talking, making nervous little gestures with his fingers, as if he were painting one of the pictures of which he spoke.

"Yes," Wilson heard him say, "they are beautiful; very, very beautiful."

He could not help thinking, as he sat there listening, that Mr. Moto was a most amazing man. Mr. Moto was talking of pictures, while Wilson was sitting doggedly, trying to match his wits against Mr. Moto, trying to gauge in his own mind how much Mr. Moto knew. It was like a bridge game when one tried to place the cards in one's opponent's hands. How much did Mr. Moto know? He suspected a great deal, but how much did he know? Wilson could only conjecture, but he was quite sure that Mr. Moto did not know as much as he did. He was very sure, for instance, that Mr. Moto did not know that Mr. Chang had left Shanghai; and the knowledge was a card in Wilson's hand. Mr. Moto might have guessed everything but he needed knowledge still. He needed definite facts and he must not learn the facts.

"If you will excuse me, please," Mr. Moto was saying, "my nation's art is something which I can understand. To me it is reality. Now with your art it is different, please. I have been to so many of your great galleries in Europe. I have tried so hard to appreciate but always there is something which eludes me. So often your artists avoid the facts, the small details, as though they were not pleasant." Mr. Moto took a sip of his whisky and smiled. "Do you avoid the facts, Mr. Hitchings? Do you, Miss Hitchings?"

The suddenness of Mr. Moto's question took Wilson off his guard. He could almost believe that Mr.

Moto had been guessing his thoughts while he had been talking.

"I try to deal with reality," Wilson Hitchings said, and Eva Hitchings did not answer.

"I am very, very glad," said Mr. Moto. "Thank you very much. Excuse me, but could I help you, Mr. Hitchings? We both think so very much. Might I ask what you are dealing with just now?"

Wilson tried to keep his own thoughts steady. When it came to matching his wits with Mr. Moto, he felt like an amateur boxer in the ring with a professional, completely aware of his lack of subtlety, and of his dullness of perception.

"Suppose you guess," he invited, "and I'll tell you if you are right."

"Thank you," said Mr. Moto. "That will be very amusing."

"I guess that you are worried, Mr. Hitchings. You are not the sort to be worried about yourself. You are worried about your Bank. I am so very, very sorry."

If Mr. Moto was not to guess too much, Wilson knew that he must tell the truth as nearly as was possible.

"Wouldn't you be worried, Mr. Moto," he inquired, "if you found that the Branch Manager of your family's banking house had mixed himself in a mess like this?"

"I should be very, very worried," Mr. Moto said. "It is very hard for you and I am very sorry. I wonder what you are going to do? Nothing, I hope that is rash, please — nothing that is foolish."

"No," said Wilson. "I am not going to do anything foolish, Mr. Moto. There is nothing I can do. Things are bad enough already. You were right when you told me to keep quietly out of this. The less I am seen in this, the better, Mr. Moto."

Mr. Moto nodded his head genially.

"Please," he said, "I am so very, very glad. So glad you see so clearly now. So glad you will do nothing foolish when you get on shore. You can see now how dangerous it is; and Miss Hitchings, she will do nothing, also?"

"Not if I can help it," Wilson said. "I hope Miss Hitchings will let me look after her."

"Please," said Mr. Moto. "I am so very, very glad. You see, everything is so very nearly finished. It has been difficult, since these men have not been very nice. I hope so much they will not trouble you after this evening. You will leave that to me, I hope. When I get ashore I wish to go completely unobserved. And now, Miss Hitchings, will you do me a favor, please?"

"What is it?" Eva asked. Wilson felt his heart give an unexpected leap. Mr. Moto had drawn a photograph from his pocket.

"Miss Hitchings, you see so many interesting people in that very interesting house of yours," Mr. Moto said. "Please, have you ever seen the man in this picture there? It would save so much trouble if you have seen him. It is the only thing of which I wish to be entirely sure."

Eva Hitchings was looking at the photograph, holding it carefully in both hands. Wilson wished to give her some signal but he did not dare. She frowned, studying the picture.

"I have seen a number of people like him," she said. "He seems very well dressed and dark. He is a rather good example of a certain type, but I don't think I have seen exactly that man before."

Mr. Moto sighed.

"I am sorry," he said, "so very, very sorry. I think he is the man who will be carrying the money. I think — but I must be sure. I must go to look, myself. And now, there is only one thing more."

"What is it?" asked Wilson Hitchings.

Mr. Moto stood up.

"When you get ashore," Mr. Moto said, "please, I beg you to do nothing. It would be very, very nice, I think, if you went quietly to your hotel and dined, but do not go near the Plantation. Neither of you, please. It will not be very nice out there to-night. They will be so very anxious to get this money on the boat. Remember, you must do nothing, Mr. Hitchings."

"Yes," said Wilson. "I'll remember."

"I am so glad," Mr. Moto said. "And now, if you will excuse me, I shall go forward to start the engine. No, please, do not bother, Mr. Hitchings. I shall need no help. Will you stand by the wheel, please? It will be growing dark in a very little while."

Mr. Moto moved away, forward, and Wilson looked at Eva Hitchings.

"Thanks," he said, "for not letting me down. Did you know the man in that picture, Eva?"

She nodded.

"Yes," she whispered. "He's the man, the one who takes the money."

"Well," said Wilson. "Moto mustn't see him. We've got to tell them, Eva. I hate it. But we've got to tell them."

CHAPTER XII

THERE was no difficulty in getting the sampan back. The cool efficiency of Mr. Moto, which seemed to make him at home in any situation, made everything move perfectly without any sense of effort.

"Thank you so much for being so polite," Mr. Moto said. "Yes, I can do many, many things. I can mix drinks and wait on table, and I am a very good valet. I can navigate and manage small boats. I have studied at two foreign universities. I also know carpentry and surveying and five Chinese dialects. So very many things come in useful. Ah, there are the lights in line. You steer so very nicely, Mr. Hitchings."

"Thanks," said Wilson. "Yes, Mr. Moto, you are a useful man."

"It is so very nice to have you say so," Mr. Moto said. "It has been a pleasure to make your acquaintance. I think I should go back to the engines, please."

Everything ran smoothly except Wilson Hitchings' thoughts and those made him hate himself because he had not been frank with Mr. Moto. He had not realized how much he had grown to like the man who was so different from himself in race and in tradition. He liked him for his courage. He liked him for his wit. And Mr. Moto trusted him — that was the worst of all. Eva Hitchings stood beside him near the wheel and her presence gave him an unexpected sense of security.

"I feel like Judas Iscariot," Wilson Hitchings said.

"Yes," she said. "I know the way you feel."

"But you understand me, don't you?" he asked.

He saw her face near his, white and shadowy in the dark.

"Do you care if I understand?" she asked.

"Yes," he said. "I do."

"I am glad of that," she answered.

He was convinced that he should not feel about her the way he did. It complicated matters and had nothing to do with actuality, but it made no difference.

"Eva," he whispered, "I am going to get you out of this. This isn't any place for you." She laughed very softly.

"You're awfully nice," she said. "It's curious, I have just been thinking that I might have to look after you."

He did not answer her because he heard Mr. Moto calling softly.

"Please, is everything all right?" Mr. Moto asked. "If you will give me the wheel, I know a dock where we can tie up. We should be alongside in a very few minutes. What a nice time we had."

"Yes," said Wilson. "Very nice. So interesting."

"So very interesting," Mr. Moto said. "Excuse me, there is one thing more I wish to ask. There is a man named Mr. Maddock. Did you see him this morning, Mr. Hitchings?"

The lights from the city rising up into the darkness of the hills came up from the harbor in a dim, faint light. Wilson hoped that the light would be faint enough so that Mr. Moto would not see him clearly.

"What makes you think I saw him?" Wilson asked.

"Please," said Mr. Moto. "I saw him this morning going to your hotel. Could you tell me what he wanted, please?"

"He came to sell me information," Wilson said. "He seemed very nervous. I didn't buy the information because I knew it already."

"Thank you," said Mr. Moto, "very much. I think you were very wise. He is not a very nice man but he is very, very capable. And now we shall be ashore in a few minutes. I can manage everything very nicely. I shall telephone you in the morning, Mr. Hitchings. Remember, keep away from the Plantation, please. You must not bother about anything. Kito will look after the men forward. Walk to the street and find an automobile and have a pleasant evening."

There was no one at the dock where they landed but Mr. Moto was very careful. He stood for a full minute examining the shadows made by the street lights.

"Good-by," whispered Mr. Moto, as he climbed up to the pier. "I must leave you now, please. It has been so very, very nice."

"Good-by," said Wilson. "Good luck, Mr. Moto."

The three of them walked together to the street which ran by the waterfront. A closed car was standing waiting at the curb and the driver was opening the door.

"Good-by," said Mr. Moto again. "I am so sorry I have so very much to do."

He stepped into the car, the door slammed, and the car moved off, while Wilson and Eva Hitchings stood staring after him.

"Now what do you think of that?" said Wilson. "He has it all arranged. We must get to the Plantation as quickly as we can. There won't be much time if he starts like that."

There was no trouble in finding a taxicab and a driver; and Wilson told the driver to hurry. As the car moved through the city, he felt as if he were at the Plantation already. He hardly noticed that Eva Hitchings was holding his hand.

"We've got to hurry," he said again.

"Yes, Wilson," she said. "We're hurrying."

"I suppose Wilkie was playing the stock market," he said. "That's the way these things always happen."

"Yes," said Eva Hitchings. "I'm afraid he was. You mustn't be too hard on him."

"I can't be," Wilson told her. "I wish to Heaven I could."

Her fingers tightened over his.

"What are you thinking about?" she asked. "I wish you wouldn't look so far away."

"I'm thinking about you," he answered. "And I wish very much I wasn't but I can't help it."

Although common sense told him it was incongruous, what he did seemed perfectly in keeping with the time and the place. Before he knew what he was doing, his arm was around her and her head was on his shoulder.

"Think about me some more," she suggested. "Maybe it will do you good. It might make you less responsible."

"Why do you like me?" Wilson asked.

"I don't know," she said.

"Well, it's the same here," Wilson said. "I don't know why I like you either. Eva, I want to tell you something. . . ."

It was true he felt less responsible. He did not seem to care much about Hitchings Brothers, or Mr.

Maddock, or Mr. Chang, or Mr. Wilkie. He had an odd sense of being himself for the first time in his life. He did not lose that feeling until they were in the mountains, passing through the gateposts of the drive that was marked "Hitchings Plantation."

"Well," said Wilson, "we are coming home."

"Yes," she said. "I am coming home. It seems as though I had never been at home until just now."

CHAPTER XIII

WILSON recalled what Mr. Moto had said the night before. He had an accurate faculty for remembering conversations.

"The only thing I need to know now," Mr. Moto had said, "is how Mr. Chang's money disappears at Hitchings Plantation and reappears in Manchukuo. I only need to know who gets it and who brings it there. Then, a few simple words over the cable to suitable persons will do the rest."

It was ironical to think that such a short while ago Wilson had been in sympathy with Mr. Moto's efforts. That was before he knew that the manager of Hitchings Brothers had involved himself in that fantastic scheme.

A few minutes before, Mr. Moto had shown him a photograph, hoping to get an answer. Clearly enough Mr. Moto was still looking for the man who had brought the money, and he had not found him yet. His search had brought him aboard the sampan, Wilson knew, and his search had not succeeded.

Wilson could guess by then that Mr. Moto never did anything without a definite reason. There was a reason for his idle conversation as he sipped abstemiously at his whisky. Wilson had watched him in a dull fascination. Mr. Moto had been trying to find out something as he talked, his restless eyes darting from face to face. Mr. Moto had been hoping to learn what both of those two strangers thought. He was painting a picture in his own mind, each line of it pitilessly accurate. His manner had been enough to tell Wilson that the picture was nearly finished.

Although it was early in the evening, only shortly after nine, the lights of the house were on full blast, casting uncertain yellow patterns against the trees and bushes around it. Halfway up the drive Wilson told the car to stop and paid off the driver. Even at that distance from the house, he could hear the music from the front room. He could not tell why the atmosphere of the place set his nerves on edge, unless it was the contrast of the music and the lights against a certain half-lost dignity. It reminded him of an old estate in the East, turned into a roadhouse or into a private school, because of death or misfortune. There was the same sadness about Hitchings Plantation in the dark — the same muted speech of better days; and yet, there was an ugliness about it too.

There was a rank, musty smell of vegetation and a feeling that unseen eyes were on them, as they walked toward the house.

"It might be better if we went in by a back door," Wilson said. "We don't want to make a scene in front."

He heard Eva Hitchings laugh.

"You're very silly sometimes," Eva said. "They probably know we are here already. There should be watchers all around the house." But her voice was very low, as though the silence depressed her. "They will be looking for Mr. Moto, don't you think?"

A moment later, Wilson saw that she was right, when a man stepped noiselessly from a clump of bamboo close by the road. There was enough light from the house by then to make him out fairly clearly.

"Why, howdy, pal," the man said. "Howdy, Miss Hitchings. Say, what the hell are you doing here? I thought you was out sailing." It was Mr. Maddock speaking. He stood in front of them as black as an undertaker, a hand in either pocket.

"We came back early, Mr. Maddock," Wilson said.

"Well, well," said Mr. Maddock. "That's interesting, pal."

"I am glad I met you," Wilson said. "Are you enjoying the evening, sir?"

"Yes," said Mr. Maddock. "It's nice I met you too, before some of the boys got rough with you. What the hell do you want here, pal?"

"Miss Hitchings lives here, doesn't she?" Wilson asked.

"Say what you want to say quick, pal," said Mr. Maddock urgently. "What's your game? Have you got the cops with you and the wagon?"

"Don't be nervous, Mr. Maddock," Wilson told him. "I'm in a hurry too. I'm in a hurry to see Mr. Wilkie. He's here, isn't he? And I'm in a hurry to see a Chinese gentleman called Mr. Chang. I take it he's here too."

Mr. Maddock made a half-audible sound in his throat.

"Wise guy, ain't you?" he said. "How the hell did you know that?"

"Never mind," said Wilson. It was plain that Mr. Maddock was startled. "I know so much that I'm frightened for you, Mr. Maddock. They've got to get that money on the boat just as quick as they can get it, see? Will you take me in to Wilkie, or do you want me to go alone?"

Then Eva Hitchings spoke. "You'd better hurry, Paul," she said. "He means it. He's worried about the Bank."

"Excuse me," Mr. Maddock said. "The big boy wouldn't miss seeing you for anything. So you was

246

worried about the Bank, was you? Excuse me, first I had better frisk you, pal. Reach up at the sky easy. No hard feelings, pal." His left hand fluttered over Wilson's pockets.

"Oh-oh," said Mr. Maddock. His hand had come upon the gunmetal revolver, and he balanced it on his palm. "Say," he said. "That's George's gun. What's the story, pal?"

"I took it away from him," Wilson said. "He was antisocial, Mr. Maddock."

"The hell you say," said Mr. Maddock.

"The hell I don't!" said Wilson. "George and the two sailors are tied up in their bunks and the boat is at the public dock. You had better get them untied quickly. You haven't got much time."

"You don't say?" said Mr. Maddock. "And where's that Jap boy, Kito?"

"I wouldn't trust him if I were you," Wilson answered. "I don't know where he is."

Mr. Maddock tapped Wilson's chest. "And you're looking for the big guy, are you?" he said. "All right, you're going to see him now, whether you like it or not. Step ahead of me, and you too, missy, through the garden to the office door. You know the way. Step lively. I knew there would be a blow-off. Didn't I say it was time to lam?"

Eva Hitchings walked first, and then Wilson and then Mr. Maddock. They walked around the house, over the path and by the overgrown garden, past the brightly lighted kitchen and then around the corner to an inconspicuous door with a window beside it. The shutters of the window were closed and the curtain was drawn, but Wilson could see a chink of light.

Someone was in the room behind the door. Mr. Maddock was knocking softly — one rap, then a pause and four short raps. The door opened a crack and he heard Mr. Maddock say: "It's okay. It's Maddock. Open up and be damn quick! This way, missy. This way, pal."

And Eva and Wilson Hitchings were standing in a small square room that was furnished like an office, and Mr. Maddock was shooting home a bolt on the door. The room was probably Eva's father's office, because the furniture was old and there were old photographs on the wall. Against the wall opposite where he was standing was a battered rolled-top desk. There was a safe beside it with its door open and half a dozen assorted chairs that must have come from other parts of the house. But Wilson remembered the furnishings only afterward. The room was stifling hot and filled with cigarette smoke and bright with electric light. Mr. Wilkie was seated near the desk, with his coat off, staring at him.

In front of the desk, in ugly business clothes, wearing a heavy watch-chain, was a placid fat Chinese, and Wilson knew who he was. He was Mr. Chang, the man he had seen for an instant in his uncle's house and the man he had seen again in Joe's Place at Shanghai. Two other men were kneeling in front of the safe. They were evidently packing neat piles of bills into a black traveling bag that lay at Mr. Chang's feet. One of them was the half-caste croupier, and the other Wilson had also seen before. He had seen him in Shanghai; a lean, cadaverous man, with dead-black hair — thin, bony features and cool white skin. There was a Russian cigarette drooping from the corner of his mouth, just as Wilson had seen it last. His narrow eyes were on Wilson and his thin forehead was creased under his black hair. It was a face that was hard to forget, a wild, relentless face. There was an instant silence as Mr. Wilkie started from his chair.

"Maddock, you damn fool!" Mr. Wilkie said. "What do you mean by this?"

Mr. Chang raised his hand and allowed it to fall gently on his knee.

"Sit down, Mr. Wilkie!" he said. His voice was high and bell-like. His enunciation was perfect. "What is it, Mr. Maddock?" Mr. Maddock gave his head a jerk toward Wilson Hitchings.

"There's plenty, boss," said Mr. Maddock. "This guy has tied up the boat at the public dock and tied up George and them two Kanakas in it. Kito's lammed, that's what." The dark-haired man got slowly to his feet.

"So," he began in a strange, foreign voice, and he leaned toward Mr. Wilkie. "So, that's what comes of your foolishness. You said he was a fool. Do you still think that he's a fool?"

"Be quiet!" said Mr. Chang. "Wait a minute, please." He picked up a telephone on the desk and called a number, and then he was speaking in Chinese, softly, swiftly, while everyone watched him without speaking, until he set down the telephone.

"That will do," Mr. Chang said. "That will be attended to. Yes, I agree with you, Sergi. It was an asinine idea of Mr. Wilkie's, and one I should have prevented, should I have known it. Maddock, bring a chair for Miss Hitchings and a chair for the gentleman! So you found them walking here, did you, Maddock? You did very well to bring them. I see you remember me, Mr. Hitchings. It is so pleasant to see one of the family here. I heard from a Mr. Stanley, in Shanghai, that you were interested in our arrangements. I have always enjoyed your uncle's conversation, and I know you will be reasonable. You have evidently come here to say something. You find us rather occupied. We are arranging to ship this money — $200,000 worth — to our poor friends in Manchuria. If you have anything to say, may I ask you to say it quickly?"

Wilson nodded toward Mr. Wilkie, who had leaned back in his chair.

"I hope you can give me just a few minutes," he said, politely. "And then you'll understand why I'm here, I think. You will if you are a reasonable man."

Mr. Chang's moonlike face curled in an easy smile and he clasped his hands across his stomach.

"My dear young friend," he said. "I have always admired the Hitchings family. You will find me very reasonable. It is my hope that we will both be very reasonable to-night. I have come here with the simple purpose of being reasonable. Pay no attention to these fellows. You and I are businessmen. What do you wish to say?"

At another time the reasonableness of Mr. Chang might have been solid and reassuring, for Mr. Chang was like a solid businessman, and an admirably fat one, from the Chinese point of view. His impassivity gave the impression of conservative reliability. But there was a quality in all that solidness which Wilson Hitchings had never encountered before. There was something adamantine behind the pale-yellow corpulence of Mr. Chang, that was as cool and as hard as the jade which his people loved. Mr. Chang's cool and emotionless glance was disconcerting. Mr. Chang was like a capable poker player, who had drawn a very good hand and who was willing to back his hand to the limit. The impact of his personality was heavy in the room, so definite that there was no doubt that it was Mr. Chang who was giving orders. When Wilson looked at Mr. Wilkie the latter avoided his glance. Mr. Wilkie was looking hot and tired, no longer cool and dapper.

"Eva, my dear," Mr. Wilkie said, "I think I had better take you to some other part of the house. This is something which you do not need to understand — something between Mr. Chang and me and Mr. Hitchings."

Eva Hitchings stood up straight.

"I would rather stay, thank you," she answered. "I'm afraid I understand everything rather well. You have been lying to me, Uncle Joe. I don't know that I blame you, but you have been lying."

"My dear," began Mr. Wilkie, "that is very inaccurate."

Mr. Chang raised a heavy blunt-fingered hand.

"That will do, if you please," he said. "I am negotiating this business, Mr. Wilkie. Miss Eva must stay with us, since she is involved. I hope she will find — pleasantly involved. No one should leave this room until we understand each other. Now, Mr. Hitchings, do not allow yourself to be interrupted, please," and Mr. Chang placed a hand on either knee and bent his head attentively forward.

Without being able to ascribe any reason for it, Wilson suddenly had a very definite wish that he was not there. Although he summoned up all his will power and self-control, he felt his confidence evaporating under Mr. Chang's cool scrutiny; because Mr. Chang was very sure of something, insolently sure of something, and Wilson did not know what. He only knew that he was caught in some combination as intricate and involved as a piece of Chinese carving.

"First, I want you to understand my reason for being here," Wilson said. "I want you to understand I am here entirely of my own free will, not because I approve of what you are doing but because I did not know until to-day that Mr. Wilkie had been extending the interests of Hitchings Brothers, without our advice or consent, Mr. Chang." He stopped and nodded at the money on the floor.

"Sergi," said Mr. Chang, "continue with the money. . . . That is very clearly put, Mr. Hitchings, I knew that you would be logical and reasonable. I was so sure of it that I wished to talk to you, until I found that Mr. Wilkie had been so impetuous as to send you out to sea. You are concerned — and naturally concerned, because you find Hitchings Brothers involved in a transaction which may hurt its reputation. You are quite right. Mr. Wilkie, as manager, has been helping more than necessary in transferring funds. It does truly involve Hitchings Brothers but I have a very high opinion of your family. You are not here to speak about recriminations and right and wrong. We both have our own interests. I presume you are here to make a proposition. What is your proposition, Mr. Hitchings?"

Wilson Hitchings kept his eyes on Mr. Chang and tried to speak coolly but there was a tremor in his voice.

"You are correct, Mr. Chang," he said. "I have come here to warn you to get this money out of here as quickly as possible and to get yourself and your messenger out with it. I don't think you have got much time. There is a Japanese agent here, Mr. Chang. He's found out everything about your methods. There is only one thing he wants. He wants to identify the man who is handling the money."

Sergi paused with a handful of currency clasped between his fingers and stared at Wilson unblinkingly.

"Ah," he said, in a silky, gentle voice. "So he has got as far as that."

"Yes," said Wilson. "He has got as far as that. . . . I do not mind about you, Mr. Sergi, whoever you may be, — I remember that I saw you in Shanghai, — or about you either, Mr. Chang; but I do mind about Mr. Wilkie. I must stop Hitchings Brothers being identified with this. That's why I'm telling you to pack up quickly and get yourselves and the money on the boat."

Mr. Chang's blunt fingers closed on his knees and relaxed but his face was impassively intent.

"Your concern is quite natural," he said. "I had the intuition that we could coöperate with one another. I even suggested it to your uncle in Shanghai. I was sorry he refused, but perhaps he will understand the necessity now. You are speaking of a Mr. Moto, I presume? I have made several attempts to be rid of Mr. Moto. Where did you see this Mr. Moto to-day? I should like to know, because we have been looking for him."

Wilson Hitchings answered deliberately.

"Mr. Moto had concealed himself in Mr. Wilkie's boat," he said. "He was in a great hurry the last time I saw him. That is why I tell you that you haven't got much time."

Mr. Chang leaned forward; his eyes were stony and unblinking.

"So that is where he was," he said. "I am deeply obliged to you, Mr. Hitchings. You have been a very great help to a useful cause to-night. Go out quickly, Mr. Maddock. You have men enough, I think. When Mr. Moto comes, bring him here. I want to be sure of everything myself. I want no error this time. Be careful with him, Mr. Maddock."

Mr. Maddock grinned and his Adam's apple moved slowly up and down.

"You want to see him here," he said, "before he gets the works?"

"Exactly," said Mr. Chang. "No one has seemed to be able to give him what you call 'the works' — certainly not last night."

"Okay, boss," said Mr. Maddock. He walked noiselessly to the door and closed it softly behind him, and the room was silent for a moment.

"Chang," said the pale man named Sergi, looking up from the traveling bag, "you had better not. This is dangerous."

"Allow me to attend to this," said Mr. Chang gently. "It is the only way for business to continue. He would do the same to you."

Wilson Hitchings opened his mouth to speak and stopped. He felt the blood drumming hotly in his ears and he heard Eva Hitchings ask the question which he had meant to ask himself.

"What are you going to do with Mr. Moto?"

Mr. Chang leaned back in his chair with his hands still on his knees.

"We will consider that in a moment," he said. "Please do not worry. Mr. Maddock is very capable in such matters. He will unquestionably bring Mr. Moto here. No doubt Mr. Moto is in the shrubbery at this very minute. You look surprised? Surely you follow me, Mr. Hitchings?"

Wilson Hitchings cleared his throat. "No," he said, "I don't."

"Pierre," said Mr. Chang. "Place a chair for Mr. Hitchings and a chair for the young lady, please. Also one for Mr. Moto — to be ready when he arrives. You know, Mr. Hitchings, really I would prefer that you sat down. Your mind will be more tranquil sitting down. I wish you to realize that we must help each other. Consider me as your elder brother, Mr. Hitchings."

In spite of himself, Wilson felt all his concentration was on the face of Mr. Chang. He tried to draw his eyes away but he could not. "You must realize that we are partners," said Mr. Chang. "You and Miss Hitchings, Mr. Wilkie and I."

Wilson cleared his throat again. He felt the perspiration gathering clammily on his forehead.

"He's right, Hitchings," Mr. Wilkie said. "Now, think and be reasonable, Hitchings."

Something inside of Wilson was struggling against his self-control — something as close to panic as anything that he had ever known.

"What do you mean?" he asked hoarsely. "If you mean I am going to be a partner in a murder, you are mistaken, Mr. Chang."

257

"Wait!" Mr. Chang's voice was very gentle. "Control yourself. You are going too far ahead. Think of yourself, Mr. Hitchings. Relax and allow the current to guide you. You have done the only thing which is reasonable and possible to-night. You have done the only thing that can save your house and that is very admirable. Your business house is very close to ruin if any of this affair is exposed. You have seen that yourself. We are not speaking of murder. We are speaking of continuing a very lucrative and patriotic business."

"Go on!" said Wilson Hitchings, and he felt his heart beating in his throat.

"That is better," said Mr. Chang, soothingly. "You are thinking of your family now and of the honor of your house. You will go far in the Orient, Mr. Hitchings. It is a good family and a good house. They will both be safe in my hands and Mr. Wilkie's, Mr. Hitchings. I can promise you that and I do not break a promise."

Wilson Hitchings tried to think, but instead he found himself struggling against a will and a determination which was stronger than his own. He tried to speak casually but he knew that he made a very bad attempt.

"You are not quite clear," he said, with difficulty. "I am trying to follow you, but you are not quite clear."

Mr. Chang nodded brightly, almost sympathetically.

"I have an admiration for you, Mr. Hitchings," he said. "You are controlling yourself very well, and so is the young lady. She will be loyal to you and you will be loyal to your house. There are many painful matters which we must face upon the road of life. I was young once myself and I appreciate your qualms. Quite beyond our own intention, we become involved in difficulties, as you are involved to-night. Then a sensible man will go forward with the tide and I know that you are sensible. If this affair becomes public, it will mean ruin to your business. You must help us so that this will not happen. You think this is the last time that we shall forward money in this manner, is it not so, Mr. Hitchings?"

"Yes," said Wilson. "Yes, I think so."

"But your reason, Mr. Hitchings," Mr. Chang continued smoothly, "will tell you that it is not so. This method of sending money is too valuable and too lucrative for us. We cannot give it up. We shall continue, because your house is so involved that it will allow us to continue." Mr. Chang paused and Mr. Wilkie spoke, confidently, like a man in a directors' meeting.

"There won't be any complications, Hitchings," he said. "There won't be a breath of scandal."

"Wait a moment," said Mr. Chang. "Wait a mo-

259

ment, please. I know the Hitchings family. They are cold and logical and Mr. Hitchings is an excellent representative. He is beginning to understand already. In a few minutes he will see that his own personal interest will be involved also — that we are partners already. I think perhaps you follow me now. I see your mind putting my words together, Mr. Hitchings. Sit quietly and think. Please do not move."

"I think you had better go on," Wilson Hitchings said. His mind was dealing with something so ugly and so sinister, and so far from his anticipations, that it took away his breath. Mr. Chang was nodding his head approvingly.

"Ah," he said. "You are a very promising young man. Anyone involved in a business transaction must be personally interested. That is why I have a surprise for you to-night. Be tranquil. Listen to me, please. Your logic must tell you that Mr. Moto must be eliminated. To-night you and Miss Hitchings will be a party in that elimination indirectly. I see you did not expect it. Quiet, Mr. Hitchings! Think! Think of yourself and the Hitchings Bank. You have been a party to it already. Of your own free will, you told us to expect Mr. Moto, Mr. Hitchings."

Wilson Hitchings sat motionless but the words were like a blow across his face. The whole business was as clear as daylight and as ugly as his thoughts.

"That's a lie!" he stammered. He was ashamed of himself for stammering. "I hadn't the least idea — "

"Of course, it is a lie!" said Eva Hitchings. "You can't do a thing like that. Do you think I'll stay here and let you do it — do you think that?"

"Wait!" said Mr. Chang softly. "One little minute please! Think, I beg you. No matter what the result will be, you will be suspected, always. Think of your family, Mr. Hitchings. And what is this man to you? He is not your affair. He will be got rid of so no one can find him. You must rely on me. Think very carefully, please. The family, Mr. Hitchings — the family."

Then Wilson Hitchings was on his feet.

"Damn the family!" he said hoarsely. "Do you think we would soil our hands with a bunch of crooks like you?"

"Sergi," said Mr. Chang, gently. "Pierre . . ."

But Wilson scarcely heard him. He had darted toward the door and his hand was on the lock. He was wrenching at the door, when he heard Eva Hitchings scream; and then her scream was choked. Then a coat was over his head and he was tripped backwards over the floor.

"Help!" Wilson shouted. "Murder!"

Even then he was shocked at the banality of his words. A knee was thrust into the pit of his stomach

261

with all the weight of Mr. Chang behind it. He was gasping, choking for his breath. Someone had his shoulders and was pulling him to his feet.

"A chair, Sergi," Mr. Chang was saying. "Tie him to the chair. Adhesive tape for the mouth, please, but I shall let him get his breath."

The coat was jerked from his head and he was staring into Mr. Chang's cool eyes.

"First a handkerchief," said Mr. Chang, "and then the tape. Can you hear me, Mr. Hitchings? You will have been here, Mr. Hitchings, and you will not have said a word. I doubt if anyone will believe your story, about being bound and gagged. You are far too much involved — but you are not a fool. Your judgment will come back."

Wilson was still struggling for his breath and there was a mist before his eyes, but he could see the room plainly enough. Opposite him, Eva Hitchings was also being tied to a chair and the croupier tied a handkerchief over her mouth. Mr. Wilkie was leaning over her.

"Eva, my dear," Mr. Wilkie was saying, "I am very sorry for all this, but it will be over in a very little while."

Sergi was tossing the pile of bank notes again into the open bag, and Mr. Chang had seated himself before the desk.

"I am so sorry," Mr. Chang said. "I hope you will

bear me no ill will, Mr. Hitchings. I think you will
thank me in the end. You will come to realize that
human life counts for less in the Orient. It may disturb you for a little while but in the end you will
forget. When we get back to Shanghai, we shall have
a talk about it, over a very good dinner. You will
sympathize with my point of view. I am essentially
a nationalist. I have no great love or respect for Japan,
but Mr. Moto, himself, will understand everything
perfectly. You need not have him on your conscience,
Mr. Hitchings. No, you need fear nothing. All you
need is a little time for quiet consideration. No one
will harm you. It is out of the question, of course.
Now, simply think of my speech in the nature of a
farewell until I return in a few hours. I telephoned
a while ago to have the sampan put in order. Sergi
and I will leave with the money. There is a vessel
outside waiting for us called the *Eastern Light*. So
you knew? I supposed you did. We need not have
any secrets any longer." He paused, and there was a
rap on the door. One long — and four short raps.

"Let them in, Sergi," said Mr. Chang. "That will
be Mr. Moto. We should have caught him in any
event, Mr. Hitchings, so do not have it any too heavily on your conscience."

CHAPTER XIV

WILSON stared at the door and felt deathly ill. Sergi had opened the door and stepped aside, revealing Mr. Moto, with his purple necktie awry and with a smudge of black earth on his cheek, walking carefully as though the ground were hot. The reason for his care was supplied by Mr. Maddock who came directly behind him, with the muzzle of a pistol pressed against Mr. Moto's back.

"Easy, pal," said Mr. Maddock. "The boss wants to see you, pal."

"Close the door, Sergi," said Mr. Chang. He paused and examined Mr. Moto, thoughtfully. "It is nice to see you, Mr. Moto," Mr. Chang said. "You have given us a great deal of trouble."

Mr. Moto bowed.

"Easy, pal," said Mr. Maddock. "Keep your hands still, pal."

"Excuse me," said Mr. Moto. His voice was as steady as ever. "I did not know you were here, Mr. Chang, though I suppose I should have guessed.

Everything has been done so very, very well — except last night you were so clumsy."

"Thank you," said Mr. Chang, gently. "I felt that circumstances demanded my management."

The gold in Mr. Moto's teeth gleamed. He was looking at Sergi with the lively interest of a professional, who forgets personal discomfort and danger in a pursuit of knowledge. Sergi looked back at him, with a cigarette still drooping from the corner of his mouth.

"How do you do, Mr. Moto," Sergi said.

"How do you do," said Mr. Moto. "I am so very, very glad to know who it has been. It is so very, very nice to know that a skillful man has been working. I hope you have been well since Mongolia."

"Yes," said Sergi. "Thank you."

"I am so very, very glad," said Mr. Moto, politely. "It is such an uncertain life. I have always respected your work so very, very much. Do you remember the code at the Naval Conference?"

The other man's face brightened and he smiled.

"Yes," he answered. "Naturally."

"You stole it so very, very nicely," Mr. Moto said. "I am so very glad to see Mr. Sergi, Mr. Chang. Now, I do not feel that I have been slow or stupid. He is so very, very clever." Mr. Moto drew his breath through his teeth. "And now I suppose," he inquired, "you are leaving for Harbin?"

"Yes," said Sergi, "in that general direction. I am a fur buyer for a London house."

"Ah, yes," said Mr. Moto. "How very, very nice. It would be so nice to know, even though it does no good."

"You are quite right," agreed Mr. Chang. "It will do no good, but of course, you understand why."

"Yes," said Mr. Moto. "Yes, of course. There is only one solution, naturally. Please do not think I am begging for any other." His glance had moved swiftly toward Wilson Hitchings. "So you did not take my advice," Mr. Moto said. "But then, I was very sure you would not, Mr. Hitchings. Please do not shake your head. All this is very natural, quite to be expected."

Mr. Chang placed his hands on his knees.

"Tie his wrists, Sergi," he said. "Gag him! You have made all the arrangements, Mr. Maddock?"

"Okay, boss," said Mr. Maddock.

"And they know where to bring him afterwards?"

"Yes, boss," said Mr. Maddock. "It's all okay."

"Do you need any help, Mr. Maddock?" Mr. Chang inquired. "I should be glad to spare Pierre to help."

"Nix," said Mr. Maddock. "I can manage him okay."

"Very well," said Mr. Chang. "I think you had better start."

"Come on, pal," said Mr. Maddock.

"Good-by, Moto," said Sergi, smoothly. "I suppose it will be my turn some day."

Mr. Moto nodded. The door opened. Standing very straight and walking carefully, Mr. Moto stepped into the dark and Mr. Maddock followed him, noiselessly. Sergi bent down and locked the traveling bag. Mr. Wilkie sat staring at the floor. Everyone seemed to be waiting for something — including Mr. Chang, who had not moved from his chair. Wilson could hear Mr. Chang's breath, smoothly and regularly. Then Mr. Chang was studying him attentively.

"Listen to me," said Mr. Chang. "In a few minutes it will be over. I know you are not a fool, Mr. Hitchings. Listen to me carefully. You and Miss Hitchings will remain here for a few hours. Mr. Wilkie will stay to look after you. He will take every care of your comfort. I shall go to see that Sergi arrives properly at the *Eastern Light*. By the time I come back, I hope you will have had opportunity to think. I hope that you will be reasonable with so much to gain and so little to lose. I shall be surprised if you are not. I shall dislike making other plans. Pierre, you shall come with us to the dock. I shall want my raincoat. Are you ready, Sergi?"

Sergi nodded, and lighted a cigarette.

"Then we have nothing to do but wait for Mr.

Maddock," said Chang. "What are you doing, Mr. Wilkie?"

"I am getting a drink, if you don't mind," Mr. Wilkie said. He opened a drawer of the desk, pulled out a bottle of whisky, drew out the cork and tilted the bottle to his lips.

Wilson waited for a sound outside. He strained his ears, but he heard no sound.

"Don't be nervous, Mr. Wilkie," said Mr. Chang. "I shall be back soon enough. I shall manage everything correctly. You must not let these matters trouble you. There are a hundred other things to do, if our friends are not reasonable. Open the door, Sergi, Mr. Maddock is knocking."

Mr. Chang rose and straightened his coat, as Mr. Maddock stepped jauntily across the threshold.

"Everything went through properly?" Mr. Chang inquired.

Mr. Maddock shrugged his narrow shoulders.

"Hell," he said. "Why shouldn't it? You didn't hear no roughhouse, did you? He croaked easy without a sound. He's on his way to take a dive over the cliff by now."

"Very good," said Mr. Chang. "You are highly satisfactory, Maddock, and now you can go out with us on the boat. You first, Sergi. I shall see you later, Mr. Hitchings."

What amazed Wilson even then in that moment of incredulous revulsion was Mr. Chang's extreme casualness. He recalled that his uncle had once told him that a foreigner could never wholly comprehend the Eastern point of view. The actions of Mr. Chang and of Mr. Moto must have been bound up in an etiquette of behavior that was admirably mixed with pride. He had seen Mr. Moto being conducted into the dark under Mr. Chang's directions, to be murdered in cold blood; yet the control of Mr. Moto and of Mr. Chang had been so perfect that there was no more emphasis on the whole affair than there might be in the exchange of ordinary social amenities. Mr. Chang had said that life was cheap, and Mr. Moto must have been in most emphatic agreement. The philosophy of those two men held something more than life. There was no doubt that manners were placed above it — manners that had placed them beyond the sickening horror which Wilson felt. He could have believed that they both would have considered his emotions uncivilized and barbaric. Mr. Chang, who had just indulged in murder, was leaving the room as calmly as a businessman might leave his office. Sergi had put on a dark hat and looked like an innocent traveling salesman. Mr. Maddock was noiseless and impersonal. He even took the trouble to lean over and pat Wilson's cheek almost affectionately, and he grinned when Wilson winced away from his cold touch.

"So long, pal," said Mr. Maddock, softly. "Seeing life, ain't you, pal?"

CHAPTER XV

THEY all were gone. They were gone like abstract thought leaving only a memory. There was still the odor of cigarette smoke in the room. Wilson was still tied in his chair, sitting mutely, facing Eva Hitchings, but the atmosphere of the room was changing into the commonplace so that Mr. Chang seemed impossible.

Wilson allowed his glance to rest on Mr. Wilkie, and it was clear that Mr. Wilkie did not share the cool assurance of Mr. Chang. Mr. Wilkie had all the attributes of a gambler who is playing for stakes that are too high for his resources. He looked old. His face was moist and drawn and there was a tremor in his fingers. He picked up the whisky bottle and took another drink, breathed deeply, and drew the back of his hand across his lips.

"You saw that?" said Mr. Wilkie, in a strained voice, and he seemed to be talking because he wanted to assure himself that he was not alone. "Eva, Eva, I am so sorry that you saw it; but listen to me, both of you. I don't like it any more than you do. You understand we are all caught in this now, don't you? You must do what he says. For Heaven's sake, do what he says!"

He seemed to expect an answer. He appeared to have forgotten that neither of them could speak.

"Listen, Hitchings," he said. "I honestly can feel for you. I am not entirely callous. I started in this because the firm's accounts got mixed; and then I could not stop. You will know why when you talk some more to that man Chang. It was my idea to have the money lost over the gaming table, and it wasn't a bad idea, but I am not a murderer any more than either of you two are. It is only because I am desperate, Hitchings.

"If you will be sensible, I promise both of you that everything will be all right. No one will ever hear a breath of this. I don't want it to come out any more than you. I am a sound man in the community and I am fond of you, Eva. I am devoted to you, even if you do not believe it.

"Please, Mr. Hitchings. Please, be reasonable. I don't know what will happen if you aren't. You've seen him; he won't stop at anything."

But Wilson Hitchings was not reasonable. He was struggling until his chair toppled and creaked.

"Don't do that!" said Mr. Wilkie. "That will do

no good. You must not do that, Mr. Hitchings."

A sound at the door made Mr. Wilkie start. Someone was rapping — one long, and four short raps — and Mr. Wilkie's mouth dropped open.

"He's back," Mr. Wilkie whispered, and his face was as white as paper. "He's changed his mind. He's back. Tell him you'll do anything he says, Hitchings! Tell him! It's your only chance!"

Mr. Wilkie's hands were fumbling with the lock in uncertain trembling haste.

"Yes," he was saying. "All right. All right."

Someone from the outside pushed the door so suddenly that it checked his speech and threw Mr. Wilkie off his balance, so that he stepped backward.

Wilson heard Eva Hitchings make a sound which was half a sob and half a groan. A small man in a dark alpaca coat bounded into the room as though he had been thrown there, and he slammed the door shut with his right hand.

"You must not make a sound please, Mr. Wilkie," he was saying. "This is Moto speaking. Mr. Chang will not be here to help you. Not ever again, I think. Yes, I am back, I am not dead. Mr. Maddock and Pierre will manage Mr. Chang and Sergi on the boat. It will be worth it to them for what there is in the traveling bag — two hundred thousand dollars. Mr. Maddock was so quick to understand. He is so very fond of money. Do you understand me, Mr. Wilkie? Mr. Chang is so rich that he has paid to have himself eliminated, I think. It was entirely my own idea."

Mr. Moto spoke politely, without undue emotion. He stood in the center of the disordered little office without ever withdrawing his eyes from Mr. Wilkie, watching Mr. Wilkie as a doctor might watch a patient, or a snake might watch a bird.

"Mr. Wilkie." His speech was slower, but his voice was carefully modulated. "Please try to understand me. Please do not let panic make you do something which you may regret. I am not bluffing, as you say in your country, Mr. Wilkie. When I say that there is nothing for you to do, I tell the truth. It is all over for you, Mr. Wilkie, but do not be alarmed. You are no concern of mine. I shall not hurt even you if you see the truth." Mr. Moto paused, still watching Mr. Wilkie. And then there was a change of attitude. All at once, Mr. Moto was no longer alert. His gold-filled teeth glittered in a smile.

"I think you believe me," Mr. Moto said. "I am so happy that you believe me. It is so much better."

Then Mr. Wilkie found his voice.

"What . . ." he began. "How did you do it?"

"Thank you," Mr. Moto said. "I shall be so glad to tell you. I manage such affairs so often. It is not very difficult. Everyone likes money. This morning I contrived to speak with Mr. Maddock. Yes, there is always someone who likes money. I even thought to approach you, Mr. Wilkie, but excuse me, I knew you were nervous but you have none of Mr. Maddock's background and experience, and excuse me, not his courage. Mr. Maddock understood me perfectly as soon as I explained. How do you say it in your own country? He was very glad to sell out for two hundred thousand dollars when he knew no questions would be asked. A part of the bargain was that Mr. Maddock should bring me here this evening. I wished to be sure who was the man carrying the money. The Russian carrier pigeon, as Mr. Maddock called him. The rest was very simple. Some of my own men seized the boat. Some former members of our Navy. There is enough fuel oil to take her into mid-Pacific. They have put a wireless aboard and I have arranged to have her met. Mr. Maddock will be landed safely in Japan together with his traveling bag. I tried so hard to keep my word, but I am so afraid that Mr. Chang and Sergi will not be there, because everything in the future will be much more simple without them. I was so glad to see Mr. Chang. I did not expect him here. I shall not bother to search you for a weapon, Mr. Wilkie, because I know you will not use it. Instead, if you have a knife in your pocket, I shall ask you to cut Miss Hitchings free and to rub her wrists carefully. I am afraid she has been tied too tight; and — will you permit me, Mr. Hitchings?"

Mr. Moto turned to Wilson Hitchings, without another glance at Mr. Wilkie, and with quick expert fingers removed the gag from Wilson's mouth. Wilson spoke with difficulty because his mouth was sore and swollen.

"It was the family," he said, chokingly. "I am sorry, Moto. I didn't think they would try to kill you." Mr. Moto was bending over Wilson's wrists.

"Please," said Mr. Moto cordially, "do not give it another thought. I should have done as you did in your place, Mr. Hitchings. I was sure that you would come here. I was so sure that you would be thinking of your family and the Bank."

"Damn the Bank!" said Wilson Hitchings. "Damn the family!"

"Please do not say that," said Mr. Moto, quickly. "Please. I counted on you to come here as quickly as possible. Your doing so has helped me very much. It has stopped them from suspecting anything, because of course you were sincere. May I rub your wrists, please, Mr. Hitchings? If I had not wished you to speak to Mr. Chang, I should have told you what I will tell you now. There will be no word from me about Hitchings Brothers, ever. Any more than there will be from Mr. Wilkie over there, if you do not lose your temper. I must depend on your discretion, please, as you must depend on mine. It is why I have been so frank. I have done so many things which are not nice and quite beyond your laws, although I hope that you are glad I did them, Mr. Hitchings."

Wilson nodded; his speech was growing clearer.

"If you ask me," Wilson said, "I think you did a fine job, Mr. Moto."

Wilson got to his feet. His legs were still numb, so that he staggered drunkenly across the room and knelt very clumsily beside Eva Hitchings. Then his arms were around her and her chestnut-colored head was on his shoulder.

"Eva," he said. "I have made an awful mess of this. I am sorry, Eva . . ."

"You needn't be sorry," he heard her answer faintly, "because I don't think you have at all."

"I said I would get you out of this," said Wilson. "Well, I am going to get you out."

She moved back her head and he saw that she was smiling. "And you said something else," said Eva. "I didn't think I would ever hear you say it. It was so sacrilegious. You said, 'Damn the family.'"

"Yes," said Wilson. "Damn the family. I have pulled them out of this hole. Mr. Wilkie, do you hear me? I am speaking to you now. You are lucky that Hitchings Brothers has a reputation. I can promise you that nothing will be said — nothing will be done, provided you will resign three months from now.

277

Not because of this, but because you are inefficient. I understand you own Hitchings Plantation, Mr. Wilkie. You will sell it to me, first thing to-morrow morning, for exactly what you paid for it. I came here to close this place, and I am going to close it. I have promised to give it back to Eva and she is going to have it, but she's going to take that sign off the gate — and I'll tell you why, Mr. Wilkie. It will come off because she promised to marry me to-night. As long as she was silly enough to promise, I think that's the best way out for everybody. . . . Don't you, Mr. Moto?"

Mr. Moto raised his hand before his lips and drew in his breath with a sibilant hiss.

"I think that is nice," said Mr. Moto, "so very, very nice."

THE END

MORE
MR. MOTO MYSTERIES!

YOUR TURN, MR. MOTO

THANK YOU, MR. MOTO

THINK FAST, MR. MOTO

Japan's most celebrated secret agent is back again in three more newly reissued Mr. Moto classic mysteries filled with intrigue, risk and romance in an Oriental setting.

AND COMING NEXT SUMMER

RIGHT YOU ARE, MR. MOTO

LAST LAUGH, MR. MOTO

Look for these at your bookstore.